WELCOME TO LARKIN

As Torn tried to get up, the big man kicked him again. The blow caught Torn flush on the cheek. His head snapped back. He fell to his hands. Another blow to the ribs sent him to the ground. The big man kicked him again and again. Torn rolled into a ball until the big man's fury was spent.

At last the blows stopped.

"Take some advice, friend," said the big man, "and keep drifting."

Torn heard the masked men mount. He heard their horses ride off, felt the ground rumble beneath his agonized body. Slowly, very slowly, he straightened himself. But pain beat him down, smashing him in waves. He tried again. He couldn't do it. The pain was too great. He dropped face first into the dirt, and everything went black.

Also by Hank Edwards

THE JUDGE
WAR CLOUDS
GUN GLORY

Published by
HARPERPAPERBACKS

HANK EDWARDS

THE JUDGE

TEXAS FEUD

HarperPaperbacks
A Division of HarperCollins*Publishers*

HarperPaperbacks *A Division of* HarperCollins*Publishers*
10 East 53rd Street, New York, N.Y. 10022

Cover illustration by Mike Wimmer

First printing: June 1991

Printed in the United States of America

HarperPaperbacks and colophon are trademarks of HarperCollins*Publishers*

10 9 8 7 6 5 4 3 2 1

CHAPTER 1

PURPLE DUSK HAD FALLEN ON THE ROLLING TEXAS hills. Thomas Fleming, judge of the U.S Fourth District Court, sat in the parlor of his small rented house, reading Jules Verne's new novel, *Around the World in 80 Days*. Fleming had met Verne in Paris, and found him a fascinating fellow. Besides, escapist stories like this helped take Fleming's mind off his troubles.

Judge Fleming's headquarters were in Madisonville, seat of Larkin County—cattle country. Strawberry Creek, which drained into the Brazos River, ran through the town. Right now, Madisonville was being torn apart by a vicious feud. The Fosters and the Larkins, the county's two biggest outfits, were at war, and every man was on one side or the other. Effective government had ceased to exist. Power belonged to masked gunmen, who rode by night,

1

killing and looting. Men were shot from ambush, or gunned down before the eyes of horrified wives and children. Travelers disappeared without a trace. Cattle and horses were stolen, stagecoaches robbed.

Fleming had tried to end the lawlessness on his own, but he had made no headway. The county residents looked on him with suspicion, if not downright hostility, because he was a Yankee. Sheriff Keegan was well meaning but ineffectual. No witnesses could be found against the killers and night riders—at least none who lived long enough to testify.

Judge Fleming was not a man to give up. If Sheriff Keegan could not bring in the wrongdoers, Fleming would use his powers under the Reconstruction Act to find a man who could. He would call in federal marshals. He would call in the army, if it came to that. He'd made his views known. There had been death threats against him, but he viewed them with contempt.

Clunk-clunk.

It was the sound of a cowbell, from out back.

"Not again," Fleming moaned. He put a marker in the book and set it on the table with exasperation. He kept a milk cow in a shed behind the house. The animal was constantly getting loose. He hoped it didn't get into his neighbor Homer Sturgis's corn field. Sturgis had threatened to sue him the next time that happened. He couldn't imagine how that would look—him, a judge, being sued. Fleming kept the cow because he liked milk with his coffee. It was a taste he had acquired during his long sojourn in Paris, where he had been part of the United States diplomatic mission. The animal had been obtained with some difficulty—few people on the Texas frontier drank milk, including the babies.

Clunk-clunk. Clunk-clunk.

Fleming rose from the crudely made chair. He was a tall, gangly man, with a long jaw and a high, domed forehead. When he walked, he was all arms and legs. Friends told him he looked like Ichabod Crane.

He paused by the back door. A pistol hung on a nail there, just in case, and he thought about taking it.

Clunk-clunk.

He forgot about the pistol. He'd need both hands just to move the cow.

He went out the door into the backyard. He smelled the fresh, new growth of spring. He looked around. The cow was nowhere to be seen. At least it wasn't in Sturgis's corn.

Clunk-clunk. Clunk-clunk.

The noise seemed to be coming from the patch of brush and woods sloping down to the creek.

Fleming followed the sound. He had to hurry before darkness fell and he lost the cow altogether.

Clunk-clunk.

He saw brush move in between the trees. "Ah ha," he said.

He plodded into the thick brush, stepping carefully. Thorns pierced his legs. "Stupid animal," he swore.

Ahead of him, the brush suddenly parted. Three masked men rose from the undergrowth, carrying pistols. One of the men held a cow bell in his hand. He clunked it mockingly.

Fleming turned to run, but he had no chance. The three men opened fire. Bullets punctured the judge's back. They split open his skull. They shattered his long limbs. He spun around and toppled into the undergrowth, dead.

2

CLAYTON RANDALL TORN ENTERED LARKIN COUNTY looking like anything but a judge. Torn was tall and lean. He'd let his blond hair grow long, and he hadn't shaved in days. He wore a rough, woolen shirt, and patched trousers were tucked into his old boots. His broken-down gray horse had cost him five dollars in Dallas. There was an old Army .44 stuck in his belt, along with his saber knife. There was nothing in his saddlebags but some supplies and a change of socks, nothing to identify him for what he was. His credentials and appointment to the Fourth District were hidden in the sole of his boot.

Torn had volunteered to be Judge Fleming's replacement. He had known Tom Fleming, and knew his wife and children, now left on their own. He thought that whoever had killed Fleming might be after his successor, as well, and he wanted to get a handle on what he was up against before announcing himself.

The road to Madisonville ran along Strawberry Creek, named after the wild strawberries growing on its banks. The country was desolate. The rolling hills, green now from the winter rains, were dotted with mesquite and clumps of cholla cactus. Not long before, this had been buffalo country, hunting grounds for Comanche and Kiowa Indians. Now the breaks and draws were filled with long-horn cattle, being fattened for market at the Kansas rail-heads. The Indian menace was gone, save for an occasional raid. Civilization was creeping in. Apparently some of these old-timers had been making their own laws for so long that they resented its intrusion.

Torn's weathered, blue eyes searched the ground to all sides of him. He couldn't shake the feeling that he'd been watched since breaking camp that morning. Ahead of him was a small hill. Five riders suddenly emerged from the fringe of post oaks at its base. Bandannas were pulled over their faces, as masks. They headed toward the road, where they split, cutting Torn's path to the front and rear.

There was a knot in the pit of Torn's stomach. The gray horse faltered, but it was too late to turn back now.

Three of the five riders reined in ahead of Torn, blocking his path, sitting their horses easily. The other two pulled in behind him.

Torn drew up and halted the gray. "Morning, gents."

"Who might you be?" inquired the riders' leader. He was a big man, with a mess of yellow curls tumbling from under his hat. Beneath the mask, Torn could see that he was bearded, as well. His horse was big and strong. It had to be, to hold that weight.

Torn's smile widened. "I might be a lot of people, but mostly what they call me is Clay Torn." He used his real name, there was no reason to suppose they'd know it down here.

"What are you doing in Larkin County?" asked the big man. His drawl had a flat, midwestern sound.

Torn shrugged. "Looking for work."

"Drifter, huh?"

"You can call it that."

"See anybody else on the trail, drifter?"

"Like who?" Torn said.

"Somebody well-dressed, official-looking—like a judge, maybe."

Torn shook his head. "Nope."

"We must have got the wrong information," said one of the riders, a tall, dark-haired man.

The big man nodded. "All right, drifter. Off your horse."

"What if I don't want to?" Torn said.

"We'll shoot you off."

He meant it. Torn dismounted.

"Search him," said the big man.

Two of the masked riders dismounted. They went through Torn's saddlebags, throwing items on the ground. "Empty your pockets," said one.

Torn did. The man took Torn's small handful of coins. He looked at them and kept them.

"Hey, wait a minute," Torn protested. "That's all the money I got in the—"

"Shut up," the big man told him.

One of the riders, a red-haired fellow, took off Torn's hat. He felt around inside the brim, and threw the hat to the ground. The other searched inside Torn's shirt and the tops of his boots. He took Torn's pistol. It was old; it didn't interest him. Then he pulled the saber knife from its sheath behind Torn's back. "Hey, lookee here." He held it up for the rest to see.

"What the hell is that?" asked the big man.

"A knife, made out of a sword, looks like," said the red-haired man.

The big man dismounted. He took the saber knife. He looked it over, felt its balance. "Where'd you get this?" he asked Torn.

"I made it," Torn said.

"What are you, some kind of blacksmith?"

"I can be a lot of things, when I have to be."

The big man cut the air with the saber knife. The blade made a whistling sound. "I like this," he said. "I like it a lot. I think I'll keep it. Thanks."

"I hadn't planned on giving it away," Torn told him.

The man's small eyes narrowed. "You fixing to take it back?"

"If I have to."

The big man hesitated. Then he said, "Oh, what the hell. Take it." He flipped the blade and offered it back, handle first, to Torn. As Torn reached for it, the big man punched him in the pit of his stomach.

Torn bent over, momentarily paralyzed, the breath driven out of him. The man followed with a clubbing blow to Torn's jaw. Torn dropped to the ground.

Dazed, Torn tried to get up. The big man was all over him, swinging with both fists. Torn grabbed the man around the waist and held on. Blows rained on his head and arms. Torn spun the man and threw him to the ground.

They grappled, rolling in the dirt. The big man tried to knee Torn's groin, missed, and got him in the thigh instead. Torn put his head down and butted the man under the chin. He heard the big man's jaws snap shut, felt his head go back. He lashed out with a right hand and knocked the big man on his back. The man's mask slipped off, and Torn had a momentary impression of a heavy, backwoods face. Torn tried to follow up his advantage, but the big man got a foot up and kicked him on the jaw. Before Torn could recover, the big man had gotten to his knees. He hit Torn square on the nose. Blood flowed. Another blow knocked Torn onto his side. He rolled over and got to his hands and knees, but the big man was already on his feet. He kicked Torn in the ribs; pain shot through his body and he cried out. The big man kicked him again. Desperate, Torn reached out. He caught the big man's foot and twisted. The big man went off balance and fell. Torn threw himself on the man's back, grabbed his hair, and began banging his head into the road, but the big man had more strength left than Torn. He rolled over, swinging a thick arm and knocking Torn off his back. The big man scrambled to his feet. His forehead was scraped raw and bleeding. As Torn tried to get up, the big man kicked him again. The blow caught Torn flush on the cheek, tearing the flesh open. Torn's head snapped back. He fell to his hands. Another blow to the ribs sent him to the ground again, lying in his own blood. The big man kicked him again and again, in the head and in the ribs. Torn tried to cover up, but it was useless. He rolled himself into a ball until the big man's fury was spent, absorbing punishment, choking on the blood in his throat, no longer feeling the pain.

At last, the blows stopped. The big man had run out of energy. Above the roaring in his ears, Torn heard the man's hoarse breathing.

"Take some advice, friend," said the big man, gasping, "and keep drifting." He took the saber knife and its Indian-beaded sheath, and put them in his own belt. He turned away. "Come on, boys."

Torn heard the masked men mount. He heard their horses ride off, felt the ground rumble beneath his agonized body. He lay there a while, trying to get to the point where it didn't hurt so much to breathe. When his breath returned to something like normal, he tried to straighten out. Pain shot through him, and he groaned. Slowly, very slowly, he straightened himself. Tears mingled with the blood and dirt on his face. When he was done, his eyes were closed and he was breathing heavily. After a minute, he was able to look around. The riders had left his horse. The animal was grazing a few yards away. There was a canteen on the horse's saddle—he had to have water. He put an arm before him, crooked a knee, and tried to crawl. The effort was more than he could bear. Pain beat him down, smashing him in waves. He tried again, but couldn't do it. The pain was too great. He dropped face first into the dirt, and everything went black.

CHAPTER 3

MADISONVILLE WASN'T MUCH OF A TOWN. ITS MOST imposing structures were the county courthouse and jail. There was a scattering of stores and saloons, with houses behind the main street. The town's primary commercial function was as a supply center for the local ranches and farmers along the creek. Some buffalo hunters outfitted there, too, the ones who didn't work out of Ft. Griffin or Adobe Walls.

It was hot on this midweek afternoon. There was little traffic on the main street, which meant few people to stare at Torn as he rode into town. Torn's battered ribs had him bent over in the saddle. The left side of his face was purple and swollen. There was dried blood on his face and shirt, from his nose and the cut on his cheek. His upper lip was puffed, and his clothes were torn. A lot of the numbness was gone from his body—he wished it would come back.

He halted the horse in front of the jail, which, like the courthouse, was built of limestone. He dismounted, grimacing from the pain. He tied up the horse and went inside.

Behind the main desk sat a smallish man with eyeglasses, chewing on a thumbnail and rooting through paperwork. The man had short, sandy hair and was in his shirtsleeves. At the sound of the door, he looked up, young and eager to please. He saw Torn and stood. "My God, what happened to you?"

"I ran into the welcoming committee," Torn told him. "Or maybe they ran into me. I'm not sure." He leaned against the desk for support. "I'm looking for the sheriff."

"I'm the sheriff. Pete Keegan." The young man pulled up a chair. "Sit down. You look like you could use a doctor."

"I could use a drink more. You don't have any whiskey, do you?"

Keegan looked him over. "This isn't a barroom. If you want a drink, you'll have to go down the street and pay for it."

Torn eased into the chair painfully. "I can't pay for it. They robbed me."

"Well, I'm sorry, but I can't help you. How about some coffee?" Sheriff Keegan went over to the small wood stove in one corner. He wet a finger and tested the coffeepot. "It's still hot." He poured some of the dark liquid into a chipped, porcelain mug and handed it to Torn.

While Torn sipped the coffee, Sheriff Keegan leaned against the desk, looking concerned. "I can probably guess what happened. You were jumped by masked riders, right?"

Torn nodded.

"Then you're lucky to be here. A lot of travelers just disappear."

"I didn't have enough on me to be worth killing," Torn said. "They only left my horse because he's too sorry to steal."

"Can you identify the men?" Keegan said.

"One of them." Torn described the big man and how his mask had come off during the fight.

Keegan shrugged helplessly. "That description fits a lot of people. Sounds like a buffalo hunter, maybe. I'll keep my eyes open."

Torn sipped more coffee. The pain in his body came and went with a pounding rhythm. "Is that all you're going to do about it?" he said.

The sheriff seemed surprised at the question. "Oh, I'll make out a report, and check the place where the incident occurred."

"It's about seven miles outside town. There's a conical hill by itself there, not far from the road."

"Kiowa Peak. I know the place. I'll look, but I can tell you now, nothing will come of it. If I find tracks, they'll split up and disappear. Even if I catch somebody and bring him in, there's no judge to try him. If I attempt to hold him, he'll be busted out before the new judge gets here. And if by some miracle I catch a suspect, and I *do* hold him, and the judge comes, you'll be murdered before you can testify."

Keegan took off his glasses and polished them with a handkerchief. "My advice to you is to forget the whole thing. Be happy you're not dead."

"You act like this happens all the time," Torn said.

Keegan held the glasses up to the light. He polished a spot that he'd missed. "Around here it does."

"What's going on?"

"A feud. Range war, some people call it."

"You mean the Larkin-Foster thing? I heard about that in Dallas, when I bought the horse. And you can't do anything to stop it?"

Keegan put the glasses back on. "Believe me, I wish I could. I'm up for re-election in the fall. For personal reasons, I'd like to stay in this area, but I'm afraid the voters are going to run me out of office, and I don't know what I'll do then."

Torn said, "How'd this feud get started, anyway?"

Keegan's eyes suddenly narrowed. "You ask a lot of questions for a drifter."

Torn sighed. He had known he would have to take someone into his confidence. He set the coffee on the desk. Slowly, painfully, he bent over and began removing his boot, gritting his teeth from the pain in his ribs.

"Hey," said Keegan, "what are you doing? This is no place to change your socks."

With a last tug, Torn got the boot off. He sat back and caught his breath. Then he reached into the boot and pulled out his credentials and letter of appointment. He smoothed them open and handed them to the sheriff. "This will explain."

Keegan read. He looked up. "Well, I'll be. . . . Why didn't you say so in the first place?" He opened the lower drawer of his desk. He pulled out a bottle of whiskey and a clean tin cup. He handed them to Torn. "I don't drink, myself. I keep this for official visitors. If I gave drinks to every drifter that wandered through that door, I'd have 'em lined up out there."

"Thanks," Torn said. He poured a drink. He tossed it down. It was cheap stuff, but he didn't care. Its raw glow took the edge off his pain. He tossed down another. He had to resist the temptation to kill the whole bottle and put himself out.

Keegan gave Torn's papers back to him. "This is great, Judge. I've been wondering when Judge Fleming's replacement would arrive. Maybe now we can make some headway against these criminals. I'll call a meeting of the town's leading citizens tonight."

"I'd like to keep this secret for a while, if you don't mind," Torn said. "That's the reason I showed up looking this way. I thought they might be waiting for me. And they were."

"They said that?"

"They talked about it."

Keegan whistled. "They have a damn good intelligence service, then. They knew you were coming before I did."

"Maybe they intercept the mail," Torn said.

"God knows," said the sheriff. "I've given up trying to figure it out. All right, Judge. We'll do it your way."

Torn poured another drink. He sipped it this time, and he grinned. "Now, maybe you'll fill me in about this feud."

Keegan cleared his throat. "Sure. It started not long after I took office. George Larkin claimed that Ed Foster was stealing his cattle. He said he'd trailed the rustled steers to Foster's range. Foster denied it, but the thefts continued. Then Foster's foreman, a man named Helpton, was ambushed and killed. Foster blamed Larkin. Next, a couple of Larkin hands were jumped along Strawberry

Creek and shot to death. The feud took off from there. Each act of violence breeds an act of revenge, which leads to still more revenge. Nothing can stop it, it's developed a life of its own. Every time it looks like it might die down, something happens to start it up again."

Keegan shook his head, "It's a shame, really. Foster and Larkin have the two biggest spreads in the county. They used to be best friends. They came out here about the same time, in the fifties, back when this was Comanche country. They fought the Indians together. At one point, when the raids were at their worst, they were the only two white families left in the county. Hell, the county's named for George Larkin. It was even sort of understood that Larkin's daughter would marry Foster's boy, Bill. Now..." Keegan shook his head. "They've turned the county into no-man's land. What the Comanches couldn't do, they're doing to themselves."

Torn brooded over his half-empty glass. "Is one side more at fault than the other?"

"Hard to say. Larkin's got more to lose. His spread's smaller, the thefts hurt him more. He thinks Ed Foster's making a play to take over the whole county."

"Is he?"

Keegan shrugged. "Maybe."

"Is Larkin the type who would kill Foster's foreman?"

"He sure never seemed to be. You can't tell about people, though."

"And Judge Fleming was killed because he tried to put an end to this?"

"That's right."

"You've no idea which faction did it?"

"No. He was found down by the stream. He was in the thickets, so he must have been lured there. He was shot—blown apart, really. I followed the killers' tracks, but they split up and gave out, like they always do."

"How come they haven't tried to kill you?" Torn said.

"Oh, they have. I've been shot at a couple of times." Then Keegan turned away. "Who am I kidding? They haven't tried to kill me. Why should they? I'm not much of a sheriff. I certainly haven't been a threat to them. I feel inadequate, helpless. I guess I'm just in over my head."

"You haven't given up, have you?"

"What? No. No, I wouldn't do that. It's just that nothing I do seems to make a difference."

Torn grinned through his puffed lip. "We'll see if we can change that."

Keegan smiled, as if Torn's remark had bucked him up. "You have anything in mind?"

"I thought maybe I'd hire out to one of the spreads, for a start. See what I can learn."

Keegan nodded. "They're always looking for hands. You'd better see Doc Goodman before you do anything. I'll lend you the money. Old Doc doesn't work for free."

Torn stood slowly, pain rippling through him. He was a good head taller than the sheriff. He took Keegan's money and finished his drink. He nodded toward the bottle. "Forget the visitors. Save the rest for medical emergencies. At the rate I'm going, I'm likely to be a frequent customer."

Torn limped toward the office door. As he did, there were hurried bootsteps on the wooden planking outside.

Torn almost ran into a breathless man in overalls, coming in the door.

The man looked past Torn. "Sheriff," he cried, "come quick. The Poker Chip Kid is drinking in the Alamo Saloon, and Bill Foster's out to get him."

CHAPTER 4

SHERIFF KEEGAN TOOK OFF HIS GLASSES. HE grabbed a shotgun and hurried for the saloon. He didn't put on a hat.

Torn kept up as best he could. It would have been easier if he hadn't been so busted up. "Who's the Poker Chip Kid?" he asked Keegan.

"Larkin's hired gun," the sheriff said. "He got here about the time the feud started. I don't know much about him. The Alamo is a Foster hangout. The Kid's either out of his mind to be in there, or he's looking for trouble."

The saloon was down the main street. *Was there a town in Texas that didn't have an Alamo Saloon,* Torn wondered. There was a crowd outside the building, clerks and store-keepers, mostly, along with a few children. A bunch of cow ponies were tied out front, swishing flies with their tails, oblivious to the excitement.

The sheriff stepped onto the rickety plank sidewalk and burst through the saloon's swinging doors. Torn followed.

"What's going on in here?" demanded Keegan, with his shotgun leveled.

Inside, the saloon was dark, narrow, and cool. There was the smell of sawdust on the floor. A man was leaning against the bar, with a group of cowhands opposite him.

The man against the bar was young. His hat hung behind him, revealing curly, blond hair and a wispy moustache. His chin-strap's slide was made of red, white, and blue poker chips. In his left hand was a schooner of beer. His right hand hung by his pistol. He grinned engagingly, but he kept his eyes on the cowboys. "Nothin' goin' on, sheriff. Just me havin' me a beer, is all."

The Foster cowhands looked ready for a fight. The sheriff turned to their leader. "Bill?"

In front of the cowboys was a tall, strong-looking man, with dark hair and thick eyebrows. He had an intense, angry face. Without taking his eyes off the Kid, he said, "Keep out of this, Pete. This fella don't belong here. He's got a big mouth. He's been calling my Pa a cow thief and a murderer, and I intend to learn him some manners."

Keegan said, "Let him finish his beer and go."

"Why?" asked the Foster boy. "Maybe he's the one backshot Joe Brune, or Tim Helpton, or one of the others. It looks like his style."

The Kid's grin faded. He pushed away from the bar. "All my men went down in front of me."

"Did they? Let's see."

Keegan stepped between them. "I said, you boys break this up."

"Sorry, Pete," said Foster. He stepped around the sheriff, facing the Kid once more.

Keegan obviously didn't know what to do. Torn tried to figure out how to interfere without breaking his cover. A real drifter wouldn't get involved in something like this.

"All right, Kid," sneered Bill Foster. "Now you'll see the trouble a big mouth gets you into."

"I don't see any trouble I can't handle," the Kid said.

"Handle this," Foster told him. He went for his gun.

"Stop it!" It was a woman's voice.

Everyone turned as the woman pushed into the room. She was of medium height. Honey-blond hair fell from under a flat, black, Spanish-style hat. She wore a white blouse, and her skirt had been slit up the middle and sewn into legs for riding. A quirt dangled from her wrist.

The bartender said, "Women ain't allowed in here, miss."

"They are now," she told him.

The Kid seemed surprised, almost embarrassed, to see her. Bill Foster clenched his strong jaw. The cowboys looked to Bill. One of them said, "Want us to put her out?"

Bill raised his hand, signaling no. To the girl, he said, "Hello, Vicky."

The girl looked at him but said nothing. She had an oval face and a healthy, outdoor complexion, with bright, blue eyes. She crossed to the Kid. "What are you doing here?"

"I was just..."

She grabbed the beer from his hand. "You've been told to stay out of this place. I can't even come into town for supplies without you going off looking for trouble. If I had my way, Father would never hire riff-raff like you. Wait for me outside."

"Yes, ma'am," said the Kid. He backed out of the saloon, keeping his eye on the Fosters, his hand near his pistol. At the door, his insolent grin returned, and he flipped a salute. "So long, boys."

"Next time I see you, you won't be this lucky," Bill Foster warned.

"That's fine with me," said the Kid. Then he was out the swinging doors.

The girl called Vicky turned to leave.

Bill Foster stood in her way. His dark face was apologetic. His voice was quiet. "It's good to see you again, Vicky."

She shook her head. "How can you say that, with all that's happened, Bill?"

He looked down. "I don't know. I like to think . . . I like to think nothing's changed between us. But I know it has."

"That's right, Bill. It has."

"I didn't want it to."

"It's a bit late for what we did or didn't want. None of us can go back."

Bill said nothing. Vicky brushed past him, and out of the saloon. Sheriff Keegan followed her. Everyone had forgotten him. "Miss Vicky?" he said. She turned.

Outside, Keegan talked to the girl for a minute. He appeared to be asking her something. She considered for a moment, then answered, smiling, apparently saying yes. Bill Foster watched them. There was a range of emotions on his face—sadness, jealousy, anger. He noticed Torn. "You," he said. "What are you looking at?"

"Me?" said Torn. "Nothing."

"Make sure you don't," Foster told him.

Torn went outside. Vicky had joined a bunch of men from the Larkin ranch, who surrounded a wagon full of supplies. One of the cowboys held a blooded roan for her, and she mounted. She cast a scorching look at the Kid, then she and her men rode out of town. The Fosters came out onto the porch of the saloon to watch them go. Tension was thick between the two groups.

Sheriff Keegan sidled up next to Torn. "Another day in Larkin County," he said, letting out his breath with relief. Then he added, "Though it would be interesting to see who'd win, if those two tangled."

The crowd began breaking up. Torn went off to see the doc. Tomorrow he would look for work.

CHAPTER 5

THE LARKIN PLACE WAS ABOUT A THREE-HOUR RIDE from Madisonville. Torn went there to look for work, and, he hoped, to find out who had gunned down Judge Fleming. The killing of the Foster foreman pointed in Larkin's direction, as did the presence of the gunman known as the Poker Chip Kid.

Torn's old, gray horse was refreshed after a good meal and a night under shelter. Torn couldn't say the same about himself. Doc Goodman had sewn Torn's cheek and put a mustard plaster on his bruised ribs. Then he had given Torn some Castoria—Castoria, like a child would take. Torn was glad he hadn't been shot. He would probably have gotten a lollipop.

The Larkin ranch lay in a long loop of Strawberry Creek.

The main house was a squat, adobe structure, with loop-holed wooden shutters, and a beamed roof covered with sod. It looked like the small fort it was.

A red-haired cowboy was standing on the gallery as Torn rode up. "Howdy," said the cowboy. He leaned against an awning post, as though holding it up. He was young, like most cowboys Torn had seen. Twenty-five was old age for them. They reminded Torn of his soldiers, during the war—not much more than children.

"Morning," Torn said. He folded his arms across his saddle horn. "Who do I see about getting a job with this outfit?"

The red-haired cowboy raised his brows, but he smiled in a friendly fashion. "Colonel Larkin and Miss Vicky do the hiring."

"A girl?" Torn said.

The cowboy laughed. "Miss Vicky's the colonel's daughter, and she can ride and shoot as good as any of us. She ain't here right now, but the Colonel's down at the corrals, getting horses ready for the round-up. Tie up your nag and I'll take you."

"Thanks," said Torn, dismounting.

The cowboy pointed to a bucket of water and a gourd suspended over it on a nail. "Drink?"

Torn dipped the gourd into the water and drank. "The boys call me Red," said the cowboy.

"I'd never have guessed," Torn said, grinning. "I'm Clay."

They shook hands and Red led Torn to the corrals. Red wore leather leggins, a wool shirt, bandanna, and a wide, shapeless sombrero. A pistol was buckled loosely around his hip. Big, Mexican spurs jingled as he walked.

"Looks like a nice spread," Torn said.

"When you ain't dodgin' bullets," Red opined.

"Indians?" Torn said.

"Fosters. They own the ranch across the creek. We're havin' a sort of war with them. Ain't you heard about it?"

Torn shook his head. "I'm not from these parts."

The corrals were alive with activity. Horses were being shod, others branded. Mustangs were being broken to the ragged cheers of onlooking men. "Here comes the colonel, now," Red said.

A tall, slim, horseman approached. He was prematurely gray, which made him look older than he was, and he had a dignified, patrician air. His white horse was as dignified as he was. He saw Red and came to a halt. The young cowboy jerked a thumb at Torn. "This here fella's lookin' for work, colonel."

"What's your name?" Larkin asked.

"Clay Torn."

Larkin's bright, blue eyes took in Torn's cuts and bruises. "You look like you've been run over by a twenty-mule team, Mr. Torn."

"Actually, there were five of them. Felt like twenty, though."

Larkin nodded. "You're a bit older than most of the men we hire."

"I can do a full day's work," Torn said.

Larkin was about to say something, when there was the sound of hoofbeats. Larkin turned and smiled. "Victoria's back."

Vicky rode up, Spanish hat hanging behind her. Torn's jaw dropped, because next to her was Sheriff Pete Keegan. The slightly built sheriff wasn't wearing his glasses. He was smiling and looking on top of the world. *Who wouldn't be*, Torn thought, *next to a girl like that.*

Larkin said, "Hello, Vicky. How was the ride?"

The girl shook back her long, blond hair. "Fine, Father. We came home for lunch, then we're going back out. I want to show Peter the view from Buzzard's Peak."

Larkin smiled at the sheriff. "You be careful, Pete, or the Fosters will accuse you of taking sides."

Keegan replied seriously. "I try to be impartial, sir. You know that."

"Yes, I can't fault you there." To his daughter, Larkin said, "You're just in time, Vicky. Here's a fellow looking for a job."

Vicky looked at Torn. "I saw you yesterday, didn't I? In the Alamo?"

"Yes, ma'am," Torn said.

Torn looked at Keegan, who nodded and said, "Mr. Torn."

"Sheriff."

"We met yesterday, as well," Keegan explained to the Larkins. "Mr. Torn was assaulted and robbed on his way to Madisonville."

"That explains the bumps and bruises," Colonel Larkin said. "Do you know anything about cattle, Mr. Torn?"

"Only what I've picked up in passing," Torn admitted.

Larkin sighed. "Can you use a gun?"

"If I have to."

Vicky cried, "Oh, Father. You're not going to hire another gunman?"

Larkin raised his gray eyebrows. "I'm sorry to say it, Victoria, but that quality has become as important as any other. Besides, men aren't exactly beating down the gates

to work here. We've lost five since the first of the year."
To Torn, he said, "Pay's thirty a month and found."

"Sounds good to me," Torn told him.

Larkin dismounted and held out his hand. "Glad to have you with us, then."

Torn took the hand. "Thanks, colonel."

Larkin eyed Torn's ramrod straight posture. "You look like a military man, Mr. Torn. Did you serve in the late war?"

"Yes, sir. Seventh South Carolina Infantry."

"Really. I was in the Third Texas, Hood's Brigade. I commanded the regiment. Our units shared many a field."

"Yes, sir."

"I recall there was a Torn in command of the Seventh Carolina. Any relation to you?"

"No, sir, not that I know." *Larkin is a shrewd bird,* Torn thought. It was a miracle they hadn't met each other before.

Larkin went on, "You might as well know, Clay, we're in bad shape here. Our cattle are being stolen faster then we can raise them. Our riders get used for target practice."

"By these Fosters that Red was telling me about?" Torn said.

Larkin nodded. "I haven't been able to put together a trail herd in two years. I have practically no money. I've borrowed against my land and stock just to pay my men, and now I can't borrow any more. If I don't get a herd through this year, I stand to lose everything. I've contracted to deliver 700 steers to Bill Watson, a trail boss out of Nueces County. Bill and his crew will take them on to Kansas. They'll be here in a week. We've got to have that herd ready."

"I understand, colonel."

"You can draw horses tomorrow. We'll give you a rifle, and I expect we've spare clothes that will fit."

Torn nodded again. "What about my horse, colonel? He's too old for this work."

"I can't afford to keep him in grain," Larkin said. "I'd hate to destroy him, but. . . ." His voice trailed off.

Torn said, "He's a good animal. Tame. There any kids you could give him to?"

Sheriff Keegan spoke up. "The Mexican woman that cooks for me has three kids. I bet they'd love to have a horse."

"There you go, then," said Larkin. "You can take him with you when you leave, Pete. Now, I have to get back to work. Vicky, see if there isn't something you can do for Clay's face before you go. After all, he's one of ours now."

Larkin saw Vicky's look, and Keegan's, and he grinned. "It will only take a few minutes. You youngsters will have plenty of time for each other."

Vicky sighed. Then she turned to Torn. "Come on."

She left her horse with Keegan and walked with Torn to the ranch house. "I see you limp, Mr. Torn. Did you get that during the war?"

"Yes, ma'am," Torn said. "Gettysburg. Just before I was captured."

"Then you spent the rest of the war in a prison camp?"

"No, ma'am. I escaped. I made my way south and re-joined my regiment."

She looked impressed. "Quite a piece of derring-do."

"It was a long time ago," Torn said.

"You don't talk like a drifter. You sound like you have education."

"A bit," Torn confessed. "Probably not as much as your father."

"My father is self-taught."

"Really?" Torn said. "He looks like one of the old planter class from before the war. A real gentleman."

"He's worked hard to get that way, believe me."

"How about you?"

"I got all my education from my mother."

"Where is she?"

Vicky looked down. "She's dead."

"I'm sorry," Torn said.

Vicky shook her head. "It's funny. When my father went to fight the war, Mother and I were left here to run the ranch. We worked the cattle as best as we could, and when the Comanches came, we fought them, right here. Four years we were by ourselves, and we survived. Then Father came home, and right after that, Mother caught pneumonia and died."

"He left you to run the ranch by yourselves?"

"Don't get him wrong. He didn't want to do it, but he believed it was his duty to go. He felt that he owed it to Texas. Ed and Bill Foster looked in on us and helped out with the ranch when they could."

"Foster didn't fight?"

"Lord, no. He didn't believe in it. The war was nothing to do with him, he said. He refused to even pay taxes for it."

Vicky turned and indicated a low rise. "Mother's buried over there. With a view of the creek and the ranch. My brothers are buried there, too. Ed—he was named for Ed

Foster—died when he was a baby. My older brother, George Jr., died of a fall from his horse. That was hard on Father, real hard. Father always wanted a son to pass the ranch on to. All he has now is me. I've had to be both son and daughter to him."

They reached the ranch house. Torn sat on the shaded gallery. "Take off your shirt," she told him.

He hesitated, and she said, "Your ribs are hurt. I can tell by the way you move. Now take off your shirt."

Torn removed the torn wool shirt. Vicky raised her eyebrows. "Look at those scars. What was your last job—target in a shooting gallery?"

"Sometimes it feels that way," Torn said.

Vicky scraped off the mustard plaster. "What a mess. Doc Goodman couldn't cure a nosebleed." She cleaned Torn up, rubbed his bruises with a mixture of camphor and snake oil, then put on some kind of hot salve that seemed to draw the pain right out of him.

"You're good with your hands," Torn said. "Reminds me of another girl."

"Your wife?"

"We would have been married, but the war got in the way. Then I lost her."

"She died?"

"Disappeared. During Sherman's march through the Carolinas. I've been searching for her ever since."

Vicky looked at him with new appreciation. "That's a long time to search. Do you think you'll ever find her?"

"I'll find her," he said.

She finished rubbing the salve on his cheek. "There." She stood. "I'm sorry if I spoke rudely about you just now."

Torn put his shirt back on. "That's all right, ma'am."

"Call me Vicky," she said. She handed him a bottle of amber liquid and a cup. "Now drink this."

Torn looked at the bottle suspiciously. "It's not Castoria, is it?"

"It's tonic. Father makes it from whiskey, medicinal roots, and herbs. I'm not sure about the roots and herbs, but the whiskey can't hurt you."

Torn grinned and took a big drink. "Thanks, Vicky."

"I'd better get back," she said. "Peter will be wondering what happened to me."

Torn said. "Isn't your riding with the sheriff going to upset Bill Foster?"

"Who cares? Bill Foster has all his father's bad qualities, and none of the good ones. He's too hot-tempered. Too quick to use a gun."

"How'd a fellow like Pete Keegan ever get elected sheriff, anyway?"

Vicky laughed. "He probably wonders about that, himself. The other candidate pulled out at the last minute. Peter won by default. No one paid much attention, then. There wasn't much more to the job than collecting taxes and filing circulars. Then the trouble started."

Vicky pointed across the ranch yard. "The bunk house is over there. Take the rest of the day off. You'll have more than enough work starting tomorrow."

Torn nodded. "I appreciate the medical attention. Be seeing you."

"Bye," she said.

Torn unsaddled and watered his gray horse, then turned him into the corral for Pete Keegan to pick up later. He carried his saddle and blankets to the bunkhouse. The

Poker Chip Kid was standing on the porch, waiting for him. The Kid smiled, but his blue eyes were hard. He moved in front of Torn as Torn came onto the porch.

"Heard you're riding with us," the Kid said.

"That's right," said Torn.

"I saw you in the saloon yesterday, and I'll tell you right now, I don't trust you. You ain't what you seem. I'll be watching you. Make a wrong move, and you're dead."

"Thanks for the welcome," Torn said.

C H A P T E R

6

THE LARKIN HANDS WERE UP EARLY NEXT MORNING.
Breakfast was biscuits, bacon, and strong black coffee.
Vicky was the cook.

Afterward, Torn was given a holster and belt for his
pistol, along with a rifle and ammunition for both. The rifle
was a Henry repeater, almost new.

"Fancy layout," he told Colonel Larkin, as he buckled
on the holster.

"The man who originally owned it didn't use it right,"
Larkin said. "He ended up dead."

Torn went to the corrals to get a horse. As the newest
man, he had the last choice. He was conscious of Larkin
and the other hands watching him as he went into the
corral. He threw his loop around a long-muscled grullo.
The horse looked peaceful enough, but Torn could tell by

the way the other hands reacted that he'd made a mistake picking him. It was too late to back out now, though. He had to ride him. These horses were supposed to be broken, but that didn't mean much. A week ago, the grullo might have been running wild and free.

Torn led the animal out. The horse had small eyes, and his ears were slightly flattened, but otherwise he showed no signs of fight. Torn bridled and saddled him and climbed on. Nothing happened. Torn relaxed just a bit. As soon as he did, the grullo exploded into a dead run. Suddenly he bucked straight up in the air and came down stiff-legged. Torn got a jolt that almost drove his spine out through the top of his head. The horse ran and bucked again, the same way. Torn was slammed into the saddle. The breath whooshed out of him. Again the horse went up in the air. Again Torn's brain was jarred loose from his skull. He felt like he'd been punched by a heavyweight. He thought his spine would turn to dust and collapse. Again the horse ran. He went into the air and came slamming back to the ground. Torn couldn't breathe, he was light-headed. He tried to hold on, but he couldn't. The horse bucked again, and Torn felt himself flying through the air.

He landed on his back. He heard the laughter of the cowboys. He lay there, wondering if his body still had all its parts.

"Is he dead?" a voice asked.

"He might've broke his back," cautioned another.

"Maybe we shouldn't have let him take that hammerhead," said a third, that sounded like Red.

Slowly, Torn got up. He staggered, dizzy. He heard more laughter, of a relieved variety this time. He saw Larkin and Vicky, looking worried. Blood ran out of Torn's nose, there was a trickle from his ear, as well. His spine felt compressed to half its normal size, and he didn't think his knees would hold him. He was getting too old for this sort of thing.

He had to get back on the horse, though. The animal stood placidly by the corrals, watching him. Torn could almost see the beast laughing. He would have liked to put a bullet in its head.

Torn took the horse's reins and mane. He swung back on. This time, he didn't give the grullo a chance to get settled. He jammed his spurs deep into the horse's flanks. As the horse took off, Torn pulled its head down and around with all his strength. The horse's legs buckled; it almost went down. Torn thought the animal might break its legs or its neck, and he didn't care. The two of them halted in a cloud of dust. Torn eased on the reins. The horse got its head up and started to run again. Again Torn pulled its head down and around, and again the horse came to a stop in a tangle of legs and dust. Torn eased up a second time. The horse straightened. It shook its head and kicked its back legs once, then trotted quietly around the corral.

Colonel Larkin came over to Torn, grinning and holding out a hand. "You'll do," he said.

Larkin divided his men into crews of three. Torn was put with Red and the Poker Chip Kid. They were assigned the northernmost part of the range. The big spring round-up was already done. Their job was to roust out prime steers and bring them to the home range for the trail herd.

"I want three-year-olds or better," Larkin told them. "No outlaws, and no walking skeletons. Don't cross Strawberry Creek and steal Foster cattle. If you find Foster cattle on our range, that's another story. They've stolen enough of our stock, you needn't be shy about changing their brands. And for God's sake, watch your backs while you're out there."

The men roped two extra horses each. They drew supplies of flour, bacon, and tools and set off. The Kid was still hostile to Torn. He got along all right with Red, but Red got along with everybody. Red was a happy-go-lucky, footloose type who let nothing bother him.

Torn was lost in thought as they rode. This was not what he had expected. Larkin had told them not to take Foster cattle, yet *somebody* had been stealing Foster's cattle. If it wasn't Larkin, who was it? Or was it just an act on Larkin's part? Maybe only Larkin and a few others were in on the secret. But if Larkin had been stealing cattle, why was he so broke? Or *was* he broke? Was that an act, too?

And who had killed Judge Fleming—and Foster's foreman Helpton, and the others?

Larkin didn't seem the type for murder, but some of the most cold-blooded killers Torn had known had been charming, well-spoken men. Had the Kid done the killings? If he had, was he acting for Larkin or on his own, for some unknown reason? Or was he acting on behalf of someone else, someone whose identity Torn could not even guess? There were plenty of men besides Larkin who would like to take over the Foster range.

Torn was glad he'd been teamed with the Kid. If the Kid wanted to keep an eye on Torn, Torn was equally determined to keep an eye on the young gunman.

They reached the northern range. They made camp beside a creek and built a pen for the cattle they expected to catch. The land on both sides of the stream was broken, filled with brushy draws and arroyos. The cattle were in the brush. The three cowhands would have to chouse them out, hold them, and drive them to the ranch.

The next morning, they began their search. They had not gone far when they came upon the remains of a fire.

Torn dismounted and sifted the ashes. "No more than a day old," he said.

All around were the tracks of horses and cattle. "Somebody's been doin' some branding here," said Red, who had also dismounted. "Two men, it looks like. And they wasn't Larkin hands."

Torn and Red remounted. The three men followed the tracks. The tracks led west, across Strawberry Creek.

The men stopped at the edge of the creek. "Foster country," said the Poker Chip Kid.

"We ain't supposed to cross," said Red.

The two of them looked to Torn. "Well, old-timer, what do you say?" asked the Kid.

"I say, let's follow them," Torn replied, and he spurred his horse into the creek.

The others hesitated, then they crossed the creek, too.

CHAPTER 7

THE THREE MEN FOLLOWED THE TRACKS OF THE STO-
len cattle. The trail led up a dry wash. Torn took the Henry
repeater from its scabbard. He levered a shell into the
chamber, and propped the rifle butt on his thigh as he
rode. Red and the Kid drew their rifles, as well, following
Torn's lead.

The tracks showed eleven head of cattle, along with the
two riders who'd taken them.

Torn's eyes never stopped moving, searching the
brushy sides of the wash. "The Foster brand is Circle F,
right?"

"That's right," said Red. "Swallow cut in the left ear."

The Larkin brand was the initials G.L. "Be hard to
change the Larkin mark to that," Torn said.

Red said, "They could always vent the brand and say the cows were sold, or they could cover it with a flatiron and rebrand. There's no bills of sale out here, and lots of cattle buyers who ain't particular."

"That what you do when you take Foster's cattle?" Torn said.

Red grinned. Even the Kid looked amused.

Red's grin faded. "You fixin' to take these fellas on, Clay?"

"Let's wait and see what happens," Torn told him.

Torn turned to the Poker Chip Kid. "You're quiet, Kid. Thought you were such a fire-eater."

"I'll eat my share when the time comes," said the Kid.

It was quiet. A whippoorwill had been crying in the brush, but now it fell silent. The men adjusted their grips on their rifles.

The wash narrowed, then leveled out. The tracks came out onto the rolling prairie. Torn and the others followed them for another quarter of an hour, then they stopped.

Two riders were coming their way.

"Is it the rustlers?" said the Kid.

Red peered closely. "It's Ed Foster, and Bill."

"You sure?" Torn said.

"I'm sure. I seen 'em enough."

The two Fosters came on. Their rifles lay across their saddles. Torn and the others waited. Torn's finger curled around the trigger of his rifle. Next to him, the Kid's horse was nervous. Torn's grullo stayed calm.

The Fosters halted about ten yards off. Ed Foster was shorter and broader than his son, with bushy eyebrows and heavy jowls, like a bulldog. He sat his horse like a block of wood. He wasn't graceful, but he was a good horseman. He scowled at the Larkin men. It appeared that he scowled a lot. "You boys are on my land," he said.

Torn sat his horse easily. He smiled. The others were content to let him do the talking, or too scared to do it themselves. "We've been chasing cow thieves," he said.

"Pretty hard to chase yourselves," old man Foster said gruffly.

Torn was unfazed. "We tracked eleven head from our range to here, along with two riders." He looked at the Fosters and counted, "One . . . two."

Bill Foster rose in the saddle, but his father motioned him to stop. "Don't play games, mister."

"I'm not playing," Torn said. "The tracks are right there, if you want to look."

Ed Foster said, "You accusing me of taking Larkin cattle?"

"Not you personally," Torn said. "I'm sure you send your flunkies to do the dirty work."

"That's a laugh," Foster said. "I've lost two dozen head of my own stock this week, that I know about."

"We didn't take 'em," Torn said.

Bill Foster leaned forward in the saddle. "One of us is lying," he said.

Torn's smile grew real friendly. "Well, it's not me. So it must be you."

Foster started to raise his rifle. Torn dropped his own rifle barrel across his left arm, pointing it at the younger Foster's chest.

"Easy," Torn said.

Ed Foster looked impressed. "You're a new man, aren't you?" he said to Torn.

"That's right. Name's Clay Torn."

"You've hooked up with a bad bunch, Mr. Torn. The Larkins killed my foreman, and three more of my hands since then."

"The way I hear it, you've been stealing Colonel Larkin's cows."

Foster snorted. "George Larkin tell you that? He's making it up. He's using it as an excuse to hide his own crimes."

"Why?" asked Torn.

"Because George missed out. He spent his life rangering and fighting Yankees and getting the county named after him, when he should have been building his spread, like me. Then one day he realized his mistake. All those years, and he had nothing to show for them. Now he's trying to make up his losses the easy way. He's selling my cows on the side, hiding the profits."

Torn said, "Do you really believe that, Mr. Foster?"

Foster's scowl deepened. "I ain't in the habit of talking to hear myself."

"Why else would Larkin hire a tinhorn like him?" asked Bill Foster, pointing at the Kid.

The Kid said nothing.

Bill looked at the Kid, and his voice rose. "Your mouth ain't so big now, is it? Is it?"

"All right, Bill," said his father.

"Let's keep this peaceful boys. After all, we got you outnumbered," said Torn.

For the first time, Ed Foster smiled. "Do you?" He motioned with his head.

Torn turned. A party of riders was approaching on their back trail.

Ed Foster said. "You didn't think we were out here alone, did you?"

The riders numbered a half-dozen. They rumbled up with a cloud of dust in their wake. Torn's eyes widened, because at their head was the big man he'd fought with two days before.

The riders halted, surrounding the Larkin men. Torn's sword knife and beaded sheath hung from the big man's belt. The big man recognized Torn, and he smiled behind his blond beard. "Well, well. Look who's here."

Ed Foster looked surprised. "You two met?"

"Informally," Torn said. "I don't believe I caught the name."

Foster said, "This is Buck Wingate, my foreman."

Wingate said, "Looks like you caught you some cow thieves, boss. Want us to string 'em up?"

Foster looked at the Larkin men and considered. Some of the horses nickered nervously. The riders tried to control them. Everybody moved easy.

Torn smiled, rifle ready. "Looks like a Mexican standoff to me."

Foster's smile matched Torn's. "You may be right. All right, you can go—this time. Next time we'll shoot first and talk later."

"Sounds fair to me," Torn said. "Adios, Mr. Foster."

Foster inclined his craggy head. His son Bill was angry; he looked like he'd just as soon shoot it out.

The three Larkin men maneuvered their horses out of the circle of Fosters, who moved aside to let them pass. Everybody was careful. One wrong move could start lead flying. When the two sides had gotten some distance between them, Torn called out, "Wingate!"

Wingate stopped. Torn jogged forward. Wingate rode out to meet him.

They halted a few feet from each other. In a low voice, so that only Wingate could hear, Torn said, "I see you still have my knife. I'll be coming for it, one day."

"I'll be waiting," Wingate said. "You know, I like this knife. It's a Union blade anyway, it ain't for a rebel like you. I had a sword, myself, during the war. While I was still in the war, that is." He laughed. "In the Forty-second Ohio, I was, officially. Mostly I was unattached. One of General Sherman's bummers."

Torn's blood went cold. It was men from the Forty-second Ohio who had destroyed his family home, where Melonie had been staying. "Were you with your regiment in South Carolina?" he asked.

"I might have been," Wingate said.

"Do you remember a plantation called Red Hill?"

"I remember what I remember."

Torn tried to control his anger. "There was a girl there—Melonie Hancock. She disappeared. I've been looking for her ever since. Do you know anything about her?"

A smile crossed Wingate's bearded face. "I'll tell you when you come for the sword."

The two men looked at each other for a long second. Then Wingate pulled on his reins and turned away.

Torn joined Red and the Kid. The three of them rode off. "For a while there, I thought we was done for. You stood up to 'em good, Clay," said Red.

"Yeah. Maybe you don't work for the Fosters, after all," added the Kid.

Torn said, "You're a genius, Kid."

Red looked anxiously over his shoulder. "Come on, let's make for our side of the creek, before the Fosters change their minds."

CHAPTER 8

THEY RECROSSED STRAWBERRY CREEK, GUIDING their horses through the willows and cottonwoods on the far side.

"How long has Buck Wingate been Foster's foreman?" Torn asked.

Red answered. "Foster hired him right after Helpton— that was the last foreman—was killed. Wingate's a bastard, but he does a good job. He gets the men to work."

"I can imagine," Torn said dryly. "Was Foster right? Did a Larkin man kill Helpton?"

"If he did, I sure don't know about it. The Fosters have been stealing our cows, but if the colonel had Helpton shot, he did it on the q.t.," replied Red.

Torn turned to the Kid.

"What are you looking at?" the Kid said. "I didn't shoot him."

"Do you know who did?"

The Kid shook his head. "Nope."

Torn's encounter with the Fosters had left him no closer to the truth. Foster had seemed genuinely aggrieved, but he could have been pretending. Had he killed his own foreman as a pretext for war with the Larkins? No, Foster wasn't the devious type. If he wanted something from you, he would come right at you.

Bill Foster, then—could he have done it, for whatever unknown reasons? But why would Bill stir up trouble with the Larkins, when he obviously liked the Larkin girl?

The Fosters were up to no good. Buck Wingate's presence on their side confirmed that. But somebody was also up to no good against the Fosters, and it had to be the Larkins. The only conclusion Torn could reach was that both sides were at fault.

Torn began to think in terms of grand juries and warrants. Judge Fleming had tried to empower a grand jury, but its members had been murdered.

That brought Torn back to his other problem. Who had killed Tom Fleming? The Fosters or the Larkins? It might not make a difference. Once Sheriff Keegan started rounding them up, somebody was likely to talk.

Unfortunately, the only crime Torn could have Keegan charge anyone with right now was Buck Wingate's assault and robbery against himself. Putting one man in jail wasn't going to end the feud, and Buck Wingate wasn't going to spill the beans just to avoid an assault charge. The most he could get for that was ninety days, and a hard case like Buck could probably do ninety days standing on his head.

The three men got back to their camp. They changed horses, then started to work. The work was hard and hot—finding steers in the brush, chasing them out, roping them, busting them in most cases to knock sense into them, then driving them to the cattle pen.

Red was a top hand. He and his horse were as one. He enjoyed the work, laughing as he matched wits with the steers. The real surprise, to Torn, was the Kid. Torn had figured him for a gunhand and nothing else, but he could ride and rope nearly as well as Red.

Torn learned the trade as he went along, and it was a painful education. Tearing into the brush after a fleeing longhorn, he was hit in the head by a tree branch and deposited butt-first into a patch of catclaw, from which he extricated himself with great difficulty.

Late that afternoon, the three cowhands returned to their camp, tired and sore, with a grand catch of five steers, which they herded into the pen. After they had grained and watered their horses and set them to graze, they ate a supper of flapjacks, fried sowbelly, and molasses.

They sat against a fallen tree, tin plates on their knees, with the grassy clearing in front of them and the springtime smells of wildflowers and huisache mingling with those of horses and cattle and strong, hot coffee.

"All this beefsteak walkin' around, and we're eatin' preserved pig," the Kid grumbled.

"Boss don't want us to eat the product," Red explained cheerfully. "Too valuable to waste on the hired help."

When they were done, they leaned back against the fallen tree. Red took out tobacco and paper, and built a smoke. "This is the life, ain't it?" he said.

He lit the cigarette and dragged on it, sighing with contentment. "Here's a question. When did you boys first really feel like men?"

Neither Torn nor the Kid answered immediately, so Red said, "Kid, I bet that's easy with you. It's when you dropped your first man, right?"

The Kid grunted, noncommittal. "What about you?" he asked Red.

Red took another drag on the cigarette. He blew out smoke, watching it dissipate on the light breeze. "It was the first time I went up the trail to Abilene. That was four years ago, back in '69."

"How old were you?" Torn asked.

"Sixteen. Man, I was some impressed with myself, too. I been up the trail twice now. Abilene is half heaven and half hell, and I don't know which half I like best. The colonel don't take cattle north hisself no more. He sells them to professional trail bosses. I thought about signin' on with one of them bosses, myself, but it'd be hard to leave the colonel now, when he's havin' all this trouble with the Fosters."

"What about you, Clay?" asked the Kid. "When did you first feel like a man?"

Torn thought for a second. "Before I fought my first duel, I guess."

"You mean a shootout?"

"No, it was a formal duel, with matched pistols, seconds, counting off paces—all that nonsense. This was in Charleston, before the war."

"What'd you fight about?" Red said.

"Fellow insulted my sister. I was young and hot-headed, and I pushed him on it."

"You kill him?" asked the Kid.

Torn looked off into some distance that only he could see. "He died of his wound two days later."

"You said you felt like a man before the duel. How'd you feel after?" persisted the Kid.

"Like a damn fool," Torn said. "That fellow didn't deserve to die, not for that. I should have kept my nose out of it and minded my own business. Even my sister said that."

"You fight any more of them formal duels?" asked Red.

"None that I care to remember," replied Torn.

They jawed a while longer, then it was time to turn in. They set a guard rotation, and Torn said, "I wouldn't advise you boys to sleep by the fire tonight."

Red raised his eyebrows. "Expectin' visitors?"

"Wouldn't be surprised," Torn said.

He gathered some brush and stuffed it in his blanket, rolled the blanket up and laid it beside his saddle with his hat on top. After a minute's hesitation, Red and the Kid did the same. Torn took his rifle, pistol, and ammunition. He found a hideout in the brush near the creek, on a piece of ground between two rivulets, and settled in there. The others followed suit, building nests on either side of the rivulets.

Torn took first guard. He was dead tired when he returned to his hideout, and fell into a deep sleep.

Sometime in the night, he became aware that the cattle were restless. The observation filtered through layers of sleep, carrying with it the message that the horses were restless, too.

Torn came awake, blinking sleep from his eyes. He rolled to one knee, reaching for his rifle. He looked out by the fire, where Red was on guard. Red had been pouring a cup of coffee, now he was staring over his shoulder, toward the shadowy brush.

Suddenly flames split the darkness. Shots exploded. Red tried to run. He took several steps, then threw up his coffee cup and fell forward, as if punched in the back by an invisible fist. Shots tore into the bedrolls by the fire. They ripped the saddles; they blasted the hats across the ground.

Torn pumped a couple of bullets in the direction of the muzzle flashes. He rolled to avoid the answering shots that ripped into the position he had just vacated. The horses were neighing, straining at their picket ropes. The penned cattle butted at the mesquite logs that penned them.

Torn fired again. By the fire, Red was on his hands and knees. He was hit again and knocked flat. He crawled feebly, trying to reach cover. Another shot smashed him down. Bullet after bullet pulped into his body, making it shake and jump with the impacts. At last, he stopped moving.

There was a crash nearby as the cattle broke down the pen and fled, bellowing, into the brush. Torn took advantage of the diversion. He made his way across the rivulet and through the undergrowth. "Kid?"

He saw the Kid, watching Red's execution with fascinated horror.

"Kid!" Torn grabbed his shoulder.

The Kid jumped in the dark and turned, with his rifle leveled.

"It's me," Torn said. Bullets were zipping into the undergrowth now, searching for them. Muzzle flashes winked like fireflies. Torn went, on, "You pin them down. I'm going to work around."

Torn started to move, but the Kid pulled his sleeve. "Clay, I can't do it. I'm scared."

"What? . . ."

"Clay, all that stuff about me being a gunman. I made it up. I never shot nobody."

Torn snapped a shot at a muzzle flash. He heard a pained oath. He pulled the Kid down. Bullets clipped the leaves around them.

"What are you talking about?" Torn said.

"I can hardly even use a gun." The Kid's words tumbled out in a torrent. "I started saying that stuff to impress people when I came west. I wanted to be a big man. I didn't know what I was getting myself into. The other day in the Alamo, I was only there to show off. I didn't think there was any Fosters in town. If Bill Foster had drawn on me, I would have been killed."

"Well, this is a hell of a time to tell me," Torn said. He levered off another shot, then hunkered down, topping off the Henry's magazine as the answering bullets came tearing in. "You got no choice, Kid. You hold 'em here, while I take 'em in the flank."

The Kid steeled himself. "I'll try."

"You better do more than try, if you want to get out of this in one piece. You got ammunition?"

"Yeah."

"Remember to move after you fire. They'll be aiming at your muzzle flashes."

The Kid nodded. Torn patted his shoulder. "All right. You're on your own."

Keeping low, Torn moved off, to the left. Behind him, the Kid raised his rifle and opened fire.

Torn crossed the rivulet. He stumbled coming up the other side. As he did, a stray bullet zipped past his nose. He stopped, and his heart missed a beat. His palms were sweating. If he hadn't stumbled, he'd be lying on the ground now, with his face splashed over the grass. He forced himself to keep going. The worst thing you could do was start thinking about it. He crossed a patch of open ground, then the rivulet on the other side. He stepped up on the bank. He bulled through the thickets, moving as fast as he could in the dark. Thorns cut his arms and legs; they sliced his hands. He angled around the line of attackers. Off to the side, the gunfire was heavy. A bobbing line of flashes showed that the attackers were moving down on the Kid. The Kid had started firing his pistol. His rifle must be out of shells. There was no time for him to reload.

Torn aimed his rifle. He began firing down the line of gun flashes. He took his time, squeezing off his shots. If he missed one target, the bullet might go down the line and hit someone else. Somebody yelled in surprise. Somebody else yelled with pain. Bullets were coming his way now, but the attackers' fire had become confused, disorganized. Torn ignored them, firing deliberately. The Kid's rifle was back in action. It looked like he was moving forward.

"Let's get out of here," somebody shouted.

There were crashes in the undergrowth, as the attackers ran. Torn's rifle was out of bullets. He drew his pistol and ran after the attackers, firing at them. The crashes grew distant, then faded. A minute later came the sound of horses galloping away.

The Kid came out of the darkness. "You all right?" Torn asked him.

"Yeah."

The two of them went back to the campfire, cautiously, in case their attackers should return. Red was dead. His body had literally been torn to pieces by bullets. He was covered with blood. The Kid looked away and was sick.

Their horses had broken loose from the picket ropes. The five steers were gone. Torn took a dead branch, lit it in the fire and began searching the brush. He found one dead man. Splashes of blood showed where more had been wounded and helped away.

Torn turned the dead man over. He held the burning branch close to his face. "This one of Foster's riders?" he asked the Kid.

"No," said the Kid. "I've never seen him before."

Torn was surprised. "You're sure?"

"I'm sure."

"Then who the hell is he?" Torn asked.

CHAPTER 9

TORN AND THE KID KEPT WATCH THE REST OF THE night, but the gunmen did not return.

At first light, they rounded up the horses. Three of the animals had been wounded by stray bullets, one of them so badly that Torn had to shoot it. The cattle were long gone, and Torn and the Kid did not look for them. They wrapped Red's body in a blanket and tied it across the back of a horse. They did the same with the gunman's body. Then they packed their supplies, saddled their own mounts, and headed back to the Larkin place.

They rode slowly, leading the extra horses. They were dead tired from chasing cattle, from the fight, and from staying up all night afterward. Their clothes were torn. Their hands were bleeding from thorn cuts. The Kid seemed about an inch taller to Torn since his confession of last night. He was more likable, too; he had shucked that false arrogance.

"For a fellow who doesn't know how to use a gun, you did a good job last night," said Torn.

The Kid shrugged. "Like you said, I didn't have a choice."

"You stick with this gunfighter routine, Kid, it's going to get you killed. Aren't you afraid somebody will call your bluff?"

"I'm real afraid," the Kid said. "I can't give it up, though."

"Why?"

The Kid hesitated. Then he lowered his eyes. "Miss Vicky," he said.

"You're fond of her?"

"More than fond."

"Love?"

"Head over heels."

"You told her?" Torn said.

The Kid shook his head, lips compressed beneath his blond moustache. "I been afraid to. She don't like me much."

"That's just my point. She might like you if she knew what you were really like."

"Yeah, but if I tell the truth, the colonel will fire me. He only hired me because he thinks I'm some kind of stone-cold killer. Anyway, I . . . I'm kind of shy."

"Well, you better get unshy quick. You've got a lot of competition for that girl."

The Kid looked at Torn sideways. "You fixin' to do some of the competing?"

"It's tempting, but I'm already spoken for. What made you pretend to be a gunfighter, anyway?"

"I don't know," the Kid said. "I thought everybody was a gunfighter out here. Been reading too many dime novels, I guess. I had no idea what the west was really like."

"Where you from?"

"Pennsylvania. Not far from Gettysburg, if you know where that is."

"I know," Torn said. "I spent a few days there, once."

The Kid's face brightened. "You might have gone right by our farm."

"Yeah."

The Kid's bright look faded. "That where you came by that limp?"

"Among other places. Why'd you come west?"

"Adventure." The Kid laughed ruefully. "I'm finding that adventure ain't all it's cracked up to be. I like this country, though. I like ranching, what I've seen of it."

"Well, good, Kid. Say, what's your real name, anyhow?"

Again the Kid hesitated. "Hans," he said at last.

"Hans?"

"Hans Schumacher. My pa's from Germany. He wanted me to have an old-country name."

Torn wrinkled his brow. "Maybe you should stick with 'Kid.'"

They got to the ranch near noon. Torn told Colonel Larkin and Vicky what had happened. The silver-haired colonel was visibly broken up. He walked away.

"He really liked that boy," Vicky told Torn.

Torn led the horse with the dead gunman's body over to Larkin. The body was already stiffening. Torn grabbed the dead man's hair and jerked the head up. "Know him, colonel?"

Larkin looked at the dead man with distaste. "No," he said. None of the other hands knew the man, either.

Torn said, "I'm not dodging work, colonel, but if you don't mind, I'd like to take this fellow to Madisonville. Maybe Sheriff Keegan can identify him."

"What difference would it make?" Larkin said wearily. "One way or the other, this fellow was connected to the Fosters."

"Maybe he was, maybe he wasn't. Maybe this'll give Keegan the opening he needs to crack this case."

"I don't think Sheriff Keegan could crack a walnut without help," said Colonel Larkin. He realized his daughter was listening, and he said, "Sorry, Vicky." To Torn, he said, "Very well. Take him in. The attack on you boys should be reported, though I doubt it'll do much good. When you get back, I'll put you with a different crew."

Before Torn left, they buried Red. They buried him on the rise, overlooking the creek, next to Larkin's wife and sons. One of the hands carved a headboard. Nobody knew Red's real name, or where he came from, though some of the boys seemed to think he was from Arkansas. In the end, the service was simple, and the headboard said, "Red. 1853–1873. A Top Hand."

CHAPTER 10

FOR THE SECOND TIME THAT WEEK, THE PEOPLE ON Madisonville's main street stopped to watch Clay Torn ride in. This time, he was leading a horse with a dead body tied across it.

Torn tied the horses in front of the sheriff's office. There was another horse already there. As Torn stepped up on the sidewalk, he heard voices through the open window. One of the voices belonged to Bill Foster, and he was angry. As Torn got closer, he heard Sheriff Keegan reply calmly. "Don't threaten me, Bill."

"It's no threat, little man," Foster said. "It's a statement of fact. Vicky's my girl. She always has been."

Torn opened the door and walked in. Keegan and Foster were alone. No deputies were around.

Foster turned and saw Torn. He scowled, just like his father. "You get around, don't you?" he said.

"You have to, if you're going to be a drifter," Torn replied equably. Then he added, "Does your father know you're here?"

"What's it to you?" Foster said.

"Just curious."

"As a matter of fact, my pa does know. He sent me."

Sheriff Keegan was absentmindedly playing with the eyeglasses on his desk. "What makes you think Vicky would have you, with the bad blood between your families?" he asked Foster.

"The bad blood ain't my doing," Foster said. "She'll have me. She loved me once, she can love me again."

Keegan's tone was faintly mocking. "She ever tell you she loved you?"

"She didn't have to. A man knows these things."

"If you boys are finished jawing, I've got something I want you to look at," said Torn.

Keegan and Bill Foster followed Torn outside. Torn showed them the gunman's body. "Look familiar?" he asked Foster.

"Should it?" Foster said.

"You tell me. You and your father were the ones making threats yesterday."

Foster shook his head. "He don't ride for us."

Sheriff Keegan looked at the body closely. "I've seen him in town a few times. Don't know who he is, though. Never had cause to find out. Why? What happened?"

"This fellow and some of his friends jumped a bunch of us last night. They killed Red. That was right after we'd had a run-in with Mr. Foster, here, and his father."

"You saying the two events are connected?" Foster said.

Torn shrugged. "If they're not, it's one hell of a coincidence."

Foster snorted. "I don't know who jumped you, mister, but it wasn't us."

"Would you admit it if it was?" Keegan said.

Foster reddened. "I don't have to listen to this." With his quirt, he pointed at the sheriff. "Just you remember what I said about Vicky." He slapped the quirt against his trousers. He mounted his horse and rode up the street.

Keegan and Torn watched him go, then Keegan hailed a boy who had been watching. He gave the boy a quarter to go for the coroner and undertaker. "In this town, they're the same person," he told Torn. He grinned. "Now there'll be more forms to fill out, so the undertaker can get his money from the county."

The two men went back inside. Keegan grew serious. "How many jumped you?"

"Ten, maybe. I was too busy dodging bullets to count."

The little sheriff shook his head. "I don't like this, Judge. It's getting too dangerous. Maybe you should just reveal yourself, and let due process take over."

Torn wrinkled his brow. "It might be more dangerous to reveal myself, if Tom Fleming was an example. Anyway, due process isn't having much luck."

"I know," said Keegan, "and it's my fault. But there's never any evidence, and every man in the county in a suspect."

"One of 'em is more than a suspect, now. I ran into the fellow that beat me up. It's Buck Wingate, Foster's foreman."

"Wingate?" Keegan looked disgusted with himself. "Of course. I should have known from that description you gave me. I just never thought that. . . ." His voice trailed off, then he said, "Well, that clears up a lot of things." He took a turn around the office. "I can arrest him if you want, but I'm thinking, if we could somehow nail him on a major charge, we might get him to talk in return for a promise of leniency."

"That's about the way I've got it figured, too," Torn said.

"I suppose it was Foster men with Wingate when he assaulted you?"

"It wasn't any of the ones who were with him yesterday. I'm pretty sure of that." Then Torn added, "Look, suppose everybody's right. Suppose that fellow out there didn't work for the Fosters. There might be a lot more to this than any of us figured."

"I don't understand," Keegan said.

"Maybe there's somebody playing both ends against the middle. Somebody whose interest it would be to stir up trouble between the Larkins and Fosters."

"Who could that be?"

"Who would benefit?" Torn said.

Keegan thought. "Grangers, maybe. They're always happy to see cattlemen killing each other. But we know that Buck Wingate is involved in this, and he works for the Fosters. In my book, Buck's a good candidate for Judge Fleming's murder. And for the stagecoach robberies, too. It looks like Larkin's right. Foster *is* trying to take over the county."

"Then who's taking Foster's cattle?"

"Nobody." Keegan had the idea suddenly, his face brightening. "Don't you see? He's making it all up, to throw suspicion off him. That's why Bill was in town just now—to report stolen cattle. They know it's nothing that can be proven. Even *they* don't know how many cattle they have."

Torn rubbed his chin. "It sounds good."

"It *is* good. Ed Foster never thought the state of Texas should have authority over him, anyway."

"There's still something about this," Torn said. "It doesn't come together, somehow. Tell you what. Why don't you nose around the farms. See if any of 'em have an unusual number of hired hands, or men who don't look like farmers."

Keegan looked doubtful, but said, "All right."

"I'm going to stay on at the Larkin place, see if I can get some hard evidence against Buck Wingate or the other Fosters."

Keegan let out his breath in frustration. "I just wish there was more I could do. You're doing all the work. You're running the risks."

Torn grinned. "That leaves you more time for Miss Vicky."

Keegan looked down, blushing. "I suppose it does." Then he grew serious. "You be careful, you hear?"

"I dealt this hand," Torn said. "I'll play it out."

CHAPTER 11

WORKING FROM DAWN TO DUSK, THE LARKIN HANDS threw together a trail herd of 700 prime steers. They drove the cattle to the home range, at the loop of Strawberry Creek, where there was good grazing. There, they would await the arrival of Bill Watson, the trail boss. All that remained was to sign the contracts, road-brand the animals, and send them on their way. Word came by advance rider that Bill Watson and his crew were a day's ride from Larkin County.

Colonel Larkin was so pleased that he ordered one of the steers slaughtered for supper. The boys applauded this welcome relief from sowbelly.

Vicky spent all day cooking stew. Along with the beef, she put in onions, corn, and canned tomatoes, as well as some Mexican spices. Her biscuits were golden brown on the outside, light and fluffy inside. The meal was topped off by dried-apple pie. The men wolfed down the food, sopping up the stew with their biscuits. Afterward they piled their plates and cups in the wash tub by the chuck wagon.

The kid went last, hanging behind the others. He shuffled his feet as he approached the wash tub. "That sure was good, Miss Vicky," he said.

"Thank you," she said coolly.

He shuffled some more. "Don't know when I last ate a meal that good. Not since my Ma's cooking."

Vicky nodded at the compliment.

The Kid looked over to Torn, who gestured him on.

The Kid cleared his throat. "Miss Vicky? . . ."

She looked up.

"I'd like to apologize for the way I acted the other day, going to the Alamo, and all. I shouldn't have done it. Besides making a fool of myself, I embarrassed you and your father."

"Well, I'm glad you realized it," Vicky said. Then she smiled. "All right. It's forgotten."

"There's one more thing I'd like to say."

"Yes?"

The Kid looked around, to make sure no one was listening. "I have to tell you." He looked once at Torn, then blurted, "Miss Vicky, all this stuff about me being a gunfighter, it ain't true. I never fired a gun in anger before last night. I never really fired one at all except for hunting."

Vicky was surprised. "Then why? . . ."

"I don't know. I was stupid. I thought I could impress people. I guess I impressed them the wrong way."

She looked at him, cocking her head slightly, as if seeing him for the first time. "Thank you for telling me."

"Don't tell your pa, will you?" the Kid said. "He'll fire me, sure."

Vicky smiled again, a full, dazzling smile. "No, he won't. And if he does, I'll rehire you. You're a good hand."

Maybe that was all the boldness the Kid had left in him, or maybe he was stunned by the intensity of her smile. "Yes, ma'am," he said. "Thank you, ma'am." He backed away, nodding. He stumbled over somebody's saddle and almost fell. Vicky couldn't help but laugh.

When the Kid got back to Torn, he was wearing a goofy smile.

"Your feet touched the ground yet?" Torn said.

"I don't think so," the Kid replied.

It was time to turn in. The men staked and saddled night horses by their bed rolls, for their turns at guard and in case of trouble. Torn picked the grullo that had given him such a hard time his first day. It was a fine, soft evening. There would be a chill before dawn, but it was warm now. The air was full of cattle smell. Torn heard the animals blowing through their noses. He heard their joints creaking, as they settled in for the night. He remained dressed save for his boots. He spread out his bedding and lay down, fingers laced behind his head, watching the clouds drift by. Around him the boys were joking, getting ready for sleep or night herd. The Kid settled in next to him, whistling to himself. He looked to Torn as a friend now, and Torn felt guilty. What would the Kid think if he knew that Torn was a bigger fraud than the Kid had ever been?

Torn saw Colonel Larkin riding around the herd, proud, with a proprietary air. In the fading light, on the white horse, with the silver hair and straight back, Larkin looked like Robert E. Lee, as Torn had once seen him beside a rural road in Maryland, watching his men as they marched to the big killing at Sharpsburg, the place the Yanks called Antietam.

As Larkin neared Torn's resting spot, Vicky joined him on her horse. The colonel beamed at her. "This is a great day for us, Victoria."

"Yes," she replied, then added, "Peter Keegan came to the house today."

"I thought I'd seen his horse. What did he want?"

"He asked me to marry him."

There was no expression on the Colonel's face. "What did you say?"

"I told him I'd think it over."

"Do you love him?"

"I don't know. He's a good man."

"He's not a cattleman."

"Neither were you, once."

The two of them rode out of Torn's earshot, still talking. Torn looked over to see if the Kid had heard. The Kid lay on his back, not moving. His eyes were open. He had heard.

Torn felt sorry for the Kid, but Vicky had to make up her own mind, and the Kid was getting a late start. It really wasn't Torn's affair. Torn turned back. He closed his eyes and fell into a deep sleep.

He was brought awake by a fusillade of gunshots. Then there was a great roar, and the earth shook. The cattle had stampeded.

It was dark. Torn dragged on his boots and ran for his

night horse. Around him, other men did the same. There was no time to figure out what the shots had been about. Torn pulled up the stake rope and threw himself on the grullo, listening at the same time to figure out which way the cattle were running. He got behind them and angled left.

He drew up onto the rear of the stampede. He'd heard enough cowboy talk to know that the way to stop a stampede was to catch the leaders and throw them into a mill. He also knew what it meant to Colonel Larkin and Vicky if this herd was lost. On Torn's right, nearly three thousand hooves drummed in furious unison. There was the occasional click of horns hitting together. Torn's horse pounded a frantic rhythm in the dark. Torn lathered the grullo for all he was worth, trusting him, having no choice. The only way to get ahead of those maddened cows was to be madder than they were. One misstep on the grullo's part could send Torn flying beneath those thundering hooves. He wondered how long he'd last if that happened. Not long enough to worry about.

Ahead, Torn glimpsed a rider in trouble, his horse down. The rider was Vicky. Out of nowhere the Kid appeared. He lifted Vicky up behind him and carried her to one side, as Torn raced by.

Torn rode faster and faster. It was an all-out dash, into the pitch-black darkness. The roaring of the cattle's hooves sounded like it was inside Torn's head, instead of outside. It seemed to be shaking his skull loose. Dust filled his eyes, clogging his nose and mouth. Suddenly there was air beneath him. His stomach went into his throat, then he hit the saddle again with jarring impact, almost slipped off and straightened himself again. Now they were climbing, and Torn realized they had gone down a gully, and were going up the other side. In this blackness, the grullo could plunge over a gorge, and Torn wouldn't know it until it was too late.

He was nearing the stampede's leaders. He could feel them, though he couldn't see them. The steers were an undulating mass in the blackness alongside him. He became aware of another rider drawing alongside, to his left. He cast a quick glance. It was the Kid. The Kid had drawn his six-gun. Torn waved him off. "No!" He doubted the Kid had heard, but maybe he'd seen the gesture. The last thing they wanted was shooting.

Torn came up on the leader's rear. He lathered his horse with the rein ends. He raced the terrified longhorn and drew even. The horse and the steer were running as one. Torn drew slightly ahead. He edged the grullo right. If this didn't work, his horse was going to have a gut full of horn. He felt the Kid fall in behind him, to guide the second leaders. He edged the grullo further right. The lead steer gave way, turning slightly. The other steers followed. Torn turned the leader more, still at full speed. Clay and the horse were leading the steers now. He took them into a wide swing, and then they were running back for the tail of the stampede.

As quickly as they had started, the leaders slowed and began to mill. Torn eased out of the mill, before he and his horse got caught in the middle of it. He'd heard stories about men who had walked out of a tightly jammed mill on the backs of the steers, but he didn't care to try it himself.

Then he was free. Other men came up to hold the cattle. The animals were milling peacefully, as if nothing had happened. Torn patted his horse's jaw. He had been glad to have the grullo tonight.

The Kid came alongside him. The two of them sat easy, catching their breaths. Their horses were lathered with sweat.

"That was the scariest ride I've ever made," said the Kid.

"Me, too," Torn said. He had new respect for the boys who took the animals up the trail and sometimes had to endure stampedes for nights on end.

"What were those shots that started it?" the Kid asked.

"I don't know. That many, they were no accident. We better go back and see."

The two of them retraced their steps in the dark. They went slowly, taking it easy on the horses.

They reached the camp, passing the deserted chuck wagon. Ahead they saw a torch. In its light were Vicky and a couple of the hands. They were gathered around a body. A riderless white horse stood nearby, and the sight sent a chill down Torn's spine.

As Torn and the Kid came up, they saw that the body was George Larkin's. They heard Vicky crying.

"You're right," the Kid told Torn. "This was no accident."

CHAPTER 12

TORN AND THE KID DISMOUNTED. TORN KNELT BE-
side Colonel Larkin. The colonel was dead, with at least
four bullet holes in him that Torn could see. The Kid stood
next to Vicky. The Kid wanted to put his arms around her,
to comfort her, but he didn't quite have the nerve. Torn
had the nerve. He drew Vicky to him, feeling her hot tears
through his shirt.

"Did anybody see who did it?" Torn asked softly.

"They didn't have to," Vicky sobbed. "It was the Fosters.
Who else could it have been? They knew Father's habits.
They knew he always rode first guard. They were waiting
for him. They couldn't miss seeing the white horse."

Torn wondered what time it was. He looked at the
Dipper, and realized with a shock that it couldn't be much
more than ten.

Vicky stood away from him. "I never thought they'd stoop this low. They planned it well, too. Kill my father and stampede the herd. That way, their chief competitor would be dead, and when I couldn't send a trail herd north, our debts would be called, and I'd lose the ranch. Then there'd be no one in the way of them running the county."

Torn said, "At least the herd's been saved. We didn't lose a one, far's I know. How about you? Are you all right?"

"I'm fine," she said. She turned. "Thanks, Kid, for saving me. My horse must have stepped in a hole. When he went down, I thought I was dead. I would have been, if you hadn't come."

The Kid looked down bashfully. "That's all right, ma'am."

Vicky cocked her head, "By the way, Kid, what's your real name?"

Torn stepped in. "I heard his real name, Miss Vicky. Trust me, you're better off calling him Kid."

A blanket was laid over the Colonel's body. A cowhand was mounted on a fresh horse and sent into Madisonville, to tell Sheriff Keegan. As the cowhand's hoofbeats faded, Torn said to Vicky, "Where did the shots come from? That stand of live oaks?"

"That's right," she said. "I was awake, I saw the flashes."

"Let's take a look around. Maybe we'll find something to tell us who it was."

"We know who it was," Vicky said. "It was the Fosters."

"I was thinking of something that might hold up in court," Torn said.

"You talk like a lawyer," she said.

Torn laughed at himself. "Yeah, I guess I do, at that."

Torn and the Kid got lanterns from the chuck wagon. Vicky joined them, as they poked around the trees and the undergrowth.

"Here's where they hid," said the Kid. "You can see the prints."

"Here's some shell casings," Torn said. He picked them up and looked at them. "From a Henry .44. That's a popular rifle—these shells could belong to anybody. They could belong to me."

They found the bootprints of seven men. Torn and the others examined the tracks. There were no odd prints, no missing heels or chipped soles, or any of the other things that identified criminals in books. There were prints of both flat heels and the new stacked heels that cowboys liked. That was it. Like the rifle shells, they could have belonged to anyone. Torn noticed that one of the men had been much bigger than the others. He wondered if it had been Buck Wingate.

They followed the footprints back to where the killers had hidden their horses. "Here's where the horse holder stood," Torn said. "Here's where they rode off."

The Kid was poking around the bushes. "Hello, what's this?"

He lifted out a pistol. It was an old Remington .44, a cap and ball model. The Kid held his lantern close to the gun. On the faded wooden grips were carved the initials "B.F."

"Bill Foster," said the Kid. "Maybe now you got something you can take to court."

"Don't jump to conclusions," Torn told him. "Those initials might just as easily mean Bud Finnegan, or Bob Fitzgerald."

Vicky took the pistol from the Kid's hand. In a soft voice, she said, "No. It's Bill's. I've seen it before. I've used it, when Mother and I fought Comanches at the house. Bill lent it to me when Father left for the war."

"I wonder how he lost it. The killers were so careful about everything else," mused Torn.

"You see how loose cowboys buckle their pistols," said the Kid. "Say Foster got on his horse. The horse maybe bucks once, and the pistol comes flying out."

Torn nodded. "Mm. And they can't find it in the dark, and they can't wait till daylight to look. It's plausible."

"It's not plausible," said Vicky. "It's what happened. Bill's going to pay for it, though."

"Let the law handle this, Vicky. There's been enough vengeance around here," admonished Torn.

Vicky hesitated, then said, "All right. I'll give the law a chance. But if there's no justice this time, I'll show this county what vengeance is really like."

It was close to first light when Sheriff Keegan arrived from town. Vicky had made coffee, and she and the men off duty stood by the fire, drinking. Keegan dismounted and went immediately to Vicky, putting his arms around her shoulders. Torn saw the Kid look away.

"Vicky," said Keegan, "this is terrible. How are you holding up?"

"All right," she said.

Keegan examined the colonel's body. He seemed to fill with resolve as he stood again. "Somehow, some way, I'm going to get the men who did this, Vicky."

"This time, you got evidence," said Torn.

He showed Keegan the pistol. He told the sheriff how they'd found it.

Keegan tapped the pistol barrel in the palm of his hand. "Finally, a break, With a good jury and a fearless judge"— his eye met Torn's—"I believe we can convict Bill Foster. And I think that when we solve this crime, we're going to solve a whole lot of other ones. Torn, would you care to join me in following the killers' trail?"

"You going to raise a posse?" Torn said.

The sheriff laughed ruefully. "No one will volunteer for a posse. There's no sense asking. They're all too scared. They're scared they'll catch somebody. They remember what happened to Judge Fleming and the members of his grand jury."

"I'd let you have some of my men, but they have to wait here and hold the herd for Bill Watson. After all this, we wouldn't want to lose the cattle now," Vicky said.

"How about if two of us go with the sheriff—me and the Kid?" asked Torn.

Vicky looked at the Kid. "All right," she said.

Keegan appeared doubtful. Vicky said, "The Kid's a good man to have with you, Peter. Take my word."

"Mine, too," Torn added.

The Kid grinned.

"All right," Keegan said. "He can come."

"We'll catch fresh horses," said Torn. "Sheriff, you get one, too. Turn yours loose with our cavvy."

The three men saddled their horses and mounted. Keegan swore in Torn and the Kid as deputies. They were ready to go.

"Be careful," Vicky told them.

"We will be," Keegan replied. To Torn and the Kid, he said, "Come on."

They rode off, following the trail of the murderers.

CHAPTER 13

THE EIGHT SETS OF TRACKS LED SOUTH. THEY
crossed and recrossed the winding Strawberry Creek. The
killers had ridden hard at first, then slowed down, apparently unworried by pursuit.

"When I was in town the other day, you talked about
checking out some of the farms, sheriff," said Torn. "Anything ever come of that?" He phrased the question carefully, because of the Kid's presence.

Sheriff Keegan shook his head. "Every place I checked
out was legitimate, though God knows, what some of those
folks are doing, trying to farm around here. This is cattle
country. There's been water in the creeks these last few
years, but wait 'til we have an old-time Texas drouth.
Those grangers'll scurry back east like fleas off a scalded
dog."

"You from Texas originally?" Torn asked him.

"Missouri, originally, but I spent most of my life in Milam County."

"Fight in the war?"

Keegan looked embarrassed. "I was in the war, but I didn't fight. I never even got near a battlefield. I was a supply officer, sort of a jumped-up clerk. No glory for me."

"No bullet holes in you, either," Torn pointed out.

They rode on and Keegan said, "Poor Vicky, I feel so sorry for her. What a horrible thing to happen. I never even had a chance to talk to the colonel about marrying her. I feel guilty about that. I should have approached him first. That's the proper way. It's just... it's just that it took me so long to work up nerve to ask her, and I wanted to know what she thought about it. Actually, I was kind of scared of the colonel, scared what he might say."

Torn saw the Kid gnawing his blond moustache in frustration. Keegan had no idea that the Kid was in love with Vicky, too. "If you and Vicky get married, are you going into the cattle business?" Torn asked the sheriff.

"I'd like to give it a try, but that's down the road. It's too early to think of those things, with all that's happened."

They rode for some miles. The country became more broken, crisscrossed by a number of small streams that fed into Strawberry Creek. Then the killers' tracks split. The eight men had gone in four different directions. Groups of two and three had gone down the small creeks. Another pair had doubled back toward the Foster place, while one man had ridden alone toward Madisonville.

"It's an old Indian trick," Torn said, "to throw off pursuit."

"Should we spilt up, or follow one trail?" asked Keegan.

"I'm for splitting up," Torn said. "There's more chance of finding something. Just in case they don't all go back to the Foster place."

"I'll take the fellow that headed for Madisonville," said the sheriff.

"Won't you lose him in all the tracks near town?" asked the Kid.

"I might get lucky," Keegan said. "Maybe they've got a hideout near town. Clay, why don't you take the ones headed back toward the Fosters? The big man is riding one of those horses. It might be Buck Wingate. The other is probably Bill Foster."

Torn smiled. "I was thinking the same thing."

"That leaves two trails for me," said the Kid. "I'll take the one with two riders. Better odds in case I run into trouble."

The men split up. Torn followed his two sets of prints back across the flowering prairie. He rode at an easy lope. The killers had made no attempt to hide their tracks.

Torn hoped he was following Wingate. He had a score to settle with the big man, and he wanted to get his saber knife back. More important, he wanted to find out what Wingate knew about Melonie.

Melonie. . . .

It had been so long since Torn had seen her. All these years, and he was no closer to finding her than he'd ever been. Would he ever find her? He'd sounded so confident about it with Vicky, but he was beginning to have doubts.

Unless Wingate knew something.

Torn took the old daguerreotype from its waterproof packet in his shirt. The picture showed Melonie in formal pose. She was wearing the embroidered, green silk gown

she'd worn on the evening he'd asked her to marry him.
Her dark hair was braided and looped in pre-war fashion.
The dress and hair style were reminders of a way of life
that no longer existed. *What must she look like now,* Torn
wondered. He gazed up at the sun. Was Melonie looking
at the same sun even now? And from where? Was Melonie
even alive? Had Torn spent a good part of his life chasing
a ghost? No. Melonie was alive. She had to be. And he
wouldn't stop looking until he had found her.

The killers' tracks dropped into a little valley. Torn
reined in on the ridge. Down below, a bearded man was
excavating a dugout. There was a covered wagon there,
along with four horses. There was a small fire going.

The bearded man looked up as Torn jogged down the
slope. "Morning," said the man. Up close, Torn saw that
beneath the long beard the man was quite young. His
clothes were worn and much mended.

"Morning," Torn replied. "You homesteading here?"

The bearded young man grinned. "Moved in yesterday.
Already got my 160 acres staked out. Name's Dane Richmond."

"Clay Torn." Torn dismounted and set his horse to
water in the stream. He took his canteen from his saddle
and drank.

"There's coffee on the fire, if you want some," said
Richmond.

"No, thanks." Torn looked around. "You got yourself a
good spot here."

"Had a better 'un picked out, closer to town. They's a
bunch of fellas pretending to farm down there, though.
Didn't look like they'd be the best of neighbors, and I sure
didn't need no trouble. I reckon I'll do well enough here."

Torn's eyes narrowed. "You say these men were *pretending* to be farmers?"

"That's right. I should know. I lived on a farm near all my life. The only crop them fellas was raisin' was trouble."

"Where is this farm?"

" 'Bout five miles south of town. It's a shame, too, 'cause it's good land. Plenty of wood and water. You can't hardly see their house. It's like they want to keep it hidden."

Torn nodded. "Don't mean to seem nosy, but I've been deputized by the sheriff. I'm following two men who were involved in a killing last night. Their tracks run right by here. Did you see them?"

"Two men?" Richmond nodded. "They come by here a few hours back. Unfriendly they was, too. Didn't so much as say good morning."

"Was one of them a big fellow, with yellow curls and a beard?"

"Yeah, that's the fellow. He was taking it easy—so's he didn't wear out his horse, I guess. That boy's a load to carry. The other fella was a redhead, with a real pasty complexion."

The second description didn't fit Bill Foster. "Could you identify the men in court?"

"If I was called to."

"You likely will be." Torn took another drink from the canteen. "What are you going to raise here?"

"Cattle," said Richmond. "My wife and baby are going to join me once I get the house done and bring in my stock. This fall, mebbe, or next spring at the latest."

Torn looked skeptical. "You'll need more than 160 acres for cattle. They'll run loose."

The bearded young man grinned. "No, they won't. I'm goin' to fence 'em in."

"There isn't enough wood for that much fencing."

"Ain't fixing to use wood. Come here." Richmond walked over to his wagon. In the wagon bed were coils of some kind of steel wire, studded with little spikes.

"Barbed wire," said Richmond. "Brand new invention. Bought it in Dallas. Feel them points."

Torn did. They were sharp.

"Ain't no cow goin' to break through this. I'm goin' to fence my range with it. That way I won't have my stock breeding with the wild 'uns. I can work on improving the breed. In a few years, I figure to make enough to buy me some other sections along here. Before you know it, I'll be a reg'lar cattle baron." He laughed at his own youthful ambition.

"Interesting," Torn said. He refilled his canteen from the creek and looped it around his saddle horn, then remounted. "Glad to have made your acquaintance, Dane. You'll be hearing about that court appearance."

"Fair enough," said the young man. "Be seeing you."

Torn rode on. He would have to tell Sheriff Keegan about the farm Dane Richmond had mentioned. Better yet, he would go there himself.

The killers' trail branched away from the Foster place. It led down a rocky, brush-filled arroyo. The tracks grew fresher. Torn was making up a lot of time on them. Too much time, it seemed. He drew his rifle from its scabbard. He stuffed a handful of extra shells in his pants pocket.

Suddenly Torn's hat was whisked off, as if by an invisible hand. Torn threw himself from his horse, even as he heard the gunshots. He landed hard on the ground and scrambled for cover behind some rocks. Bullets kicked up dirt around him. He heard his horse neighing with pain.

He dived behind the rocks, as bullets whined off them. He took a quick look up and saw puffs of smoke hovering in the still air.

There were two men, high up, one on each side of the arroyo. One was firing what sounded like a Sharps .45, the other was using a Henry repeater, like Torn's own. Torn swore at himself. The killers had turned around and ambushed him, and he'd ridden right into it, like the greenest kid. It was a miracle he was still alive. His horse lay in the arroyo's bottom, thrashing in agony.

There was a shot. A bullet screamed off nearby rock. Torn wasted a shot in the direction of the smoke, even though he didn't have a good target. He wanted them to know he could fight back.

He looked around. He had a good spot here, covered by rocks on three sides. Unless he did something stupid, the two gunmen wouldn't be able to get a clear shot at him without exposing themselves.

Two more shots whined harmlessly off the rock. Torn saw movement up the hillside. Somebody was trying to work closer. Torn aimed, fired. The movement stopped. Torn heard an angry oath. Then a voice cried, "It ain't worth it. Let's get out of here."

Two figures moved off, dodging among the rocks. The first was a stocky redhead. The second was Buck Wingate.

For a second, Torn had a clear shot at Wingate's broad back. He aimed. His finger curled around the trigger.

Then he stopped. Sweat poured down his forehead. What was he doing? He couldn't kill Wingate, not until he knew the truth about Melonie. He needn't kill Wingate, anyway, much as he would have liked to. With Dane Richmond's testimony, he could take care of Wingate the proper way, in court. He might even be able to break Wingate's whole gang.

The two gunmen disappeared. Torn heard the sound of retreating horses.

Torn stood. He walked over to his horse. The animal was kicking weakly. He'd been struck in the breast. There was no hope for him. Torn drew his pistol. He put the barrel to the horse's head and fired. The horse jumped once, then lay still. Torn holstered his pistol wearily. This was the part he'd hated most about the war, the pain and suffering and death that was inflicted on innocent animals. Now the war was over, but the animals were still suffering.

Torn found his hat. There was a neat hole in the crown. He'd come that close to death. He put the hat on. He dragged his saddle from the dead horse and threw it over his shoulder. With the rifle in his other hand he began to walk. He'd go back to Dane Richmond's place and borrow a horse from him.

It was a long walk. Torn was tired and his feet were sore by the time he topped the rise that led down to Richmond's place. Then he stopped. He dropped the saddle, and he brought the rifle up, ready to fire.

Richmond's dugout had been caved in. His wagon was overturned and smashed; his horses were gone. A body lay near the wagon.

Torn moved down the slope. There was no one around. Only an eerie silence. Dane Richmond lay in a contorted position, reflecting the agony he must have gone through. His bearded face was blue; his swollen tongue protruded. Around his neck, biting into it and drawing blood, was the length of barbed wire with which he had been strangled.

CHAPTER 14

DANE RICHMOND'S STRANGLER HAD BEEN A STRONG man. He must have been, to have bent the stiff, barbed wire around Richmond's throat. The heavy rawhide gloves that he'd worn for the job lay beside the settler's body. Richmond had been tortured before he'd been killed. There were bruises and welts on his body. There were also long, deep cuts. Torn's saber knife would have made cuts like that. By the look of the ground, Richmond had put up quite a struggle before giving in.

Torn buried Richmond, wrapping the young man's battered body in his canvas wagon cover. He made a crude cross of sticks, tied with rawhide. He said a silent prayer over the grave and vowed to bring the men who had done this to justice.

He searched the dead man's meager belongings for an address where he could write to the widow, but found nothing. The poor woman might never learn what had happened to her husband. She might spend months, even years, waiting for word from him. Eventually, she would start a long search. Like Torn's search for Melonie.

Torn found a pencil and a piece of paper. He left his saddle at the wrecked campsite, with a note on it, stating that the saddle belonged to the GL Ranch. Then he started walking, heading for Madisonville.

Torn blamed himself for Dane Richmond's death. He blamed himself for making Richmond's wife a widow, for making his child an orphan. If he had pulled the trigger on Buck Wingate when he'd had the chance, Richmond would still be alive. In that case, Torn might have no chance of learning about Melonie. But had the information about Melonie—if indeed there was any—been worth an innocent man's life? Had it been worth shattering the lives of the man's wife and child?

What did Torn have to show for his mistakes? He had followed the tracks of George Larkin's killers. He could identify Buck Wingate as one of the men who had ambushed him. He could infer—but not prove—that the tracks he'd followed had been made by Wingate. His only witness to that was dead, and Ed Foster would likely have a dozen men ready to swear that Wingate had been on the ranch all last night and today. The same with Bill Foster. Torn had Foster's pistol. He could prove it was Foster's pistol, but he couldn't prove that Foster had carried it last night. Foster could always say he'd lost it. Somebody must have picked it up. Another dozen "witnesses" would swear that Bill Foster at had been at the ranch house, or in town, when the murder took place. Torn's evidence was circumstantial. It wouldn't hold up in any court of law, much less his own.

"Damn," he said, and he kicked a rock, hard enough to hurt his toe.

He wanted to go to the farm that Dane Richmond had talked about. He had an idea that the farm, and its occupants, fitted into the picture, but he didn't know how.

He heard a noise behind him. He turned to see a farm wagon, pulled by two mules, and driven by a skinny man with a patch over his left eye.

The wagon drew even with Torn. The one-eyed man was of indeterminate age—he might have been thirty or fifty, or anywhere in between. His eye patch was dirty and ragged at the edges—like the man himself. The wagon rode alongside Torn for a piece. Neither man spoke.

"Bit of a limp you got there," the one-eyed man said at last.

"I was born with one foot shorter than the other," Torn told him.

"Don't that bother you none?"

"Only when I walk on level ground."

"You're dressed like a cowhand. Where's your horse?"

"Got himself poisoned."

"Alkali?"

"Lead."

"Heading for town?"

"I could be."

"Care to ride?"

"I can't pay."

"That's all right. You tell lies about your leg, I'll tell 'em about my eye."

Torn grinned. "Sounds fair to me."

The man braked the wagon. Torn climbed up. He extended his hand. "Clay Torn."

"Herb Penner," said the one-eyed man. He flicked the reins, starting the wagon again. The mules plodded along.

"So what happened to your eye?" Torn said.

Herb Penner chuckled and winked his good eye. "I tell everybody I got it at Gettysburg, at Pickett's Charge. I tell 'em I was the last man back from the Yankee lines."

"And the truth is?"

"I got it riding cattle down in the *brasada*, the brush country. It was the damndest thing. We was chasin' cattle after dark. I followed this one critter into the brush. Well, you know what the brush's like, thicker than flies on a Mexican breakfast. I'm riding full tilt, blind 'cause of the dark, and I took the business end of a palo verde branch straight in my eye. After that's when I decided to take up farming."

"Do you know anything about a farm about five miles south of Madisonville? Kind of a run-down place?"

"You must mean the Wingate place," Penner said.

"Wingate?" Torn said.

"Yeah. Ed Foster's foreman, Buck Wingate, he owns it. Don't know what for, and frankly, I ain't asking. Not with that crowd he keeps there. Why you want to know?"

"Just wondering. Heard it was good land. Thought it might be for sale."

"Mister, take my word. It ain't. Don't look for no hospitality there, neither. You see that place, you ride on by."

Torn nodded.

"Now, where'd you get that limp?"

Torn looked at him. "Pickett's Charge."

*   *   *

Sheriff Keegan was in his office when Torn got there. Keegan had been in the saddle most of the night and a good part of the morning. Behind his glasses, his eyes were red-rimmed with fatigue. He was surprised when Torn told him about the ambush. About Dane Richmond, and Richmond's fate, he wasn't as surprised.

"God," he said, "will it ever end?"

Torn poured himself some coffee. "What happened to your trail?"

Keegan shrugged. "It worked out like the Kid said. I lost the fellow's tracks among all those on the road into town. Whoever I was tailing, he didn't go back to the Foster place. Oh, well, it was worth a try."

Torn eased his weary body into a chair. His spine ached from being bounced on the seat of Herb Penner's springless wagon. He drank the coffee. "Any Foster riders in town?"

Keegan shook his head. "No. I looked. Haven't been any all day. Leastways, nobody's seen any."

Torn didn't tell Keegan about Wingate's farm. The sheriff was trying so hard to do something right. He might go haring out there and get himself killed.

"Are you going to swear out warrants for Wingate and Bill Foster?" Keegan said.

"I'd prefer to wait," Torn told him. He explained his misgivings about the case. "I don't want to issue warrants until we have evidence that will hold up in court."

"What about Wingate? You've got him on attempted murder."

"I only had a back view of him, and there will be plenty of men to swear he was somewhere else at the time of the ambush. If you were an impartial juror, who would you believe?"

Keegan sighed. "Where does that leave us?"

Torn swallowed some more coffee. "It leaves me looking for a horse. I've got to get back to the ranch."

"I'll go with you. I want to hear what the Kid found. Do you really trust that fellow?"

"Yes," Torn said.

Torn rented a horse at county expense. He and Pete Keegan rode back to the Larkin ranch. It was late afternoon when they got there. Bill Watson's trail crew had arrived, and the herd was being road branded. Vicky was watching the process from horseback, with Watson. When she saw Torn and Keegan approach, she left the trail boss and rode out to them.

"Where have you two been? We've been worried about you," she said. "Clay, that's not the horse you rode out on."

"No, ma'am," Torn said. He told her about the ambush.

"Was it bad?" she said.

Torn grinned. "It was good practice, in case I have to get my old job back—target in a shooting gallery."

The Kid was cutting out steers to be branded. He turned the work over to someone else and rode out to Torn and the Sheriff.

"Did you find anything?" Keegan asked him.

The Kid looked chagrined. "I lost the trail. It died out in a dry wash. I couldn't pick it up again. Whoever those fellows were, they'd swung back north, toward the Foster place."

"Or toward town," Torn said. "Or near it."

"Yeah," said the Kid.

"What are you driving at?" Pete Keegan asked Torn.

"Nothing. Just thinking out loud."

Torn looked toward the herd. "They're almost done," he said to Vicky.

Vicky nodded. "The ranch has been saved. Father would have been happy. I only wish he could have been here to see it." She looked down. "We'll bury him tomorrow."

"The ranch is yours now," Torn said.

"Yes," she said.

"It's a big responsibility."

"I'm a big girl."

Vicky quirted her horse back toward the branding. The three men watched her.

"She's got guts," said Pete Keegan admiringly.

"She'll need luck to go with it," Torn said.

"Maybe we can help her with that part," said the Kid. He spurred his horse and rode after her.

CHAPTER 15

COLONEL LARKIN'S FUNERAL WAS THE NEXT DAY. A grave had been dug on the low rise, next to the three others. A large crowd had come from Madisonville and the surrounding area. They had left horses, buggies, and wagons at the bottom of the hill. The men stood around the grave bareheaded; the women wore bonnets. Beside the grave was the casket, covered with the Texas flag. There was an honor guard of Confederate veterans, brandishing an assortment of rifles. Below the site was a sweeping view of Strawberry Creek and the ranch. In the distance could be seen the dust of the departing trail herd.

Vicky stood at the head of the grave. She wore a white dress, the only dress she owned. Beside her were Sheriff Pete Keegan and the trail boss, Bill Watson, a south Texas brushpopper with an enormous moustache, who had remained behind his herd for the funeral. Torn, the Kid, and the rest of the ranch hands stood behind them.

The preacher, a young man who knew the colonel mostly by reputation, was speaking:

"Lord, we remember today thy servant, George Arthur Larkin, who did so much for this county, and for the state of Texas. When George first came to this country, Lord, the only inhabitants were pagan red Indians. The lush pastures around us, now home to the cattle that feed a nation, were overrun by wandering buffalo. . . ."

There was a stir in the audience. People turned their heads.

Across Strawberry Creek rose a cloud of dust.

"It's the Fosters," somebody said. "The Fosters are coming."

People began whispering, pointing. The preacher tried to go on, but no one was listening, and he gave up.

Torn could make out the riders now. Ed and Bill Foster were in the lead. Some two dozen of their hands were behind them. Around Torn, men nervously licked their lips, wondering if there was to be trouble.

"No sense running," Torn said in a steady voice. "Our firearms are back at the ranch buildings. We'd never make it. Best we just sit tight."

The riders came boiling across the creek and up the rise. Ed and Bill Foster wore dark suits, so did a few of the others. The rest wore clean shirts and trousers. All were unarmed. They halted and dismounted their blowing horses, leaving them with Buck Wingate. Wingate saw Torn looking at him, and he grinned contemptuously. It was all Torn could do not to go after the big man right there.

The Fosters came forward, followed by their men. White with rage, Vicky moved down the rise to confront them. "How dare you show your faces here?" she rasped.

Ed Foster drew up his hulking form. "We come to pay our respects, Vicky," he growled. "Maybe me and George ain't got along in recent years, but I still counted him as a friend."

"Is that why you killed him?" Vicky asked. "My God, I'd hate to see how you'd treat an enemy."

"Vicky, we had nothing to do with your father's death," Bill Foster said.

"Then why did we find your pistol at the scene?" she demanded. "It was the old Remington, the one you lent me during the war."

There was a stunned murmur from the crowd. Ed Foster rounded on his son, who backed up and said, "I lost that pistol, Pa. I didn't kill the colonel."

"You was out that night," the old man rumbled.

"I was with. . . ." Bill glanced at Vicky, "I was with that Mexican whore, Angela Maria. Ask her, if you don't believe me. I swear, I lost that pistol last week. Or maybe it was stolen. I don't know what happened to it."

Vicky's voice filled with disgust. "I expected more from you, Bill."

The young man reached out. "Vicky, you got to . . ."

"Don't touch me. Don't talk to me."

Ed Foster watched, and the scowl dropped from his face. He seemed to grow older before Torn's eyes. He let out a deep sigh. "Where did we all go wrong, Vicky? Hell, I used to bounce you on my knee. I looked on you as my own daughter."

"You went wrong when you started this feud. You went wrong when you killed my father."

Ed Foster bristled. "You forget who killed my foreman, Helpton."

"The Larkins had nothing to do with that."

"And we had nothing to do with. . . ." Bill Foster said.

"I don't believe you," Vicky interrupted. "When you killed Father, you thought you could run off our herd and bankrupt me, but you didn't. The ranch is safe now."

Ed Foster recovered his composure. "You'll never be able to run it, Vicky, a slip of a girl like you. I'd always hoped that you and Bill. . ." He toed his boot in the dust. "Anyway, I'm prepared to make you an offer for your house, your stock, and your grazing rights. A more than generous offer, I might add."

"You can't buy me out, Ed Foster."

"Vicky, I think you should. . ."

Torn stepped forward. "You heard her, Mr. Foster. She isn't selling."

Bill Foster looked at Torn with hostility. "You seem to do a lot of the talking for this outfit lately."

"Maybe I got a big mouth," Torn said.

"Maybe somebody should shut it for you," Bill said.

"Maybe somebody should try."

Bill moved forward.

"Bill!" said his father. "This isn't the time for that. We're here to pay our respects to an old friend."

"Pay them, then, and leave," said Vicky.

Ed's heavy jaw worked. "You won't make it here," he warned Vicky. "You'll be busted by Christmas."

Then Ed removed his hat and walked up to the casket. He stared at it, in silence. If he wasn't sincere, it was a hell of a good act, Torn decided. The old man was followed, one by one, by Bill and the rest of his men. They were like warriors, saluting a fallen foe whom they respected.

While this was going on, Torn wandered down the rise, to where Buck Wingate waited with the horses.

Wingate grinned behind his blond beard, revealing large, greenish-brown teeth. "Enjoy your walk the other day, Torn?"

"You'd be surprised how informative a good walk can be," Torn replied.

Wingate's grin widened. "You done a fine job with that sawed-off pig sticker. I been having a nice time with it."

"Yes," Torn said. "I saw the results. I want to know about Melonie Hancock, Wingate."

"Like I said, I'll tell you that when you come for the sword."

"When I come for it, you'll wish I hadn't," Torn told him.

The Fosters returned. Torn stepped aside as they mounted their horses. Ed Foster nodded formally to Vicky, then he and his men rode away, back across Strawberry Creek.

CHAPTER 16

THE SERVICE WAS OVER.

The honor guard fired its salute, using an assortment of rifles. The flag-draped casket was lowered into the grave. Vicky Larkin tossed a symbolic handful of dirt on top, then the diggers spaded the rest of the earth into the grave. Later, the headboard would be pounded into the ground with the flat blade of a shovel.

The large crowd paid its respects to Vicky, then broke up, the men and women headed for their various homes. At last, all were gone save for Vicky, Pete Keegan, and the Larkin ranch hands.

The cowboys stood hesitantly, with their hats in their hands. One of them, Bryce Harwood, the longest-serving hand, stepped forward.

"Miss Vicky, me and the boys got something to say."

"Yes?" Vicky said.

Harwood looked around, as if for support. Then he said, "Well, ma'am, we took a vote last night, and . . . and we're quitting."

"All of you?"

"All but two."

There was a pause, then Vicky said, "Who are the two?"

"Me," said the Poker Chip Kid.

"And me," said Clay Torn in a low voice. Torn's eyes met briefly with Sheriff Keegan's.

Vicky looked at the others, disappointment visible on her face.

"It's nothing personal, Miss Vicky, and it's not 'cause we don't want to work for no woman. But we're cowhands, not soldiers. And with Colonel Larkin dead, we . . ."

"You don't feel it's safe any more," Vicky said.

"No, ma'am."

"You think the Fosters will come down hard on us?"

"Yes'm, we do. And, no offense to Sheriff Keegan, here, but we don't think he can stop it. I like you, Miss Vicky— we all do—but it's over. Old man Foster was right. You ain't going to make it here. Ranchin' ain't a woman's trade. We think you should take Foster's advice. Sell this place and get out, while you can."

"I'll never sell," Vicky said. Then she softened. "I can't blame you men, I suppose. I'm actually surprised you've stuck by us this long. It'll be hard at first, but we'll hire more men."

Bryce Harwood's voice was apologetic. "Begging your pardon, ma'am, but I don't think you will, not from this county. Everybody's too scared to sign on with you."

"Then we'll get them from another county," she said.

Harwood said nothing. Nor did anyone else. Everyone knew the difficulty of the task that lay before Vicky.

Harwood said, "No hard feelings, Miss Vicky?"

"No," Vicky said. "No hard feelings. You men have all been paid?"

They nodded. "We'll get our things from the bunkhouse and be going," Harwood said.

The Kid stepped forward. "One thing," he told them.

They turned.

"Don't take no jobs with the Fosters. That could be dangerous to your health."

"Don't worry," said Bryce Harwood. "We ain't quittin' here to go work for them snakes. Good-bye, Miss Vicky."

"Good-bye," she said.

Each of the men shook Vicky's hand, then left for the bunkhouse.

Pete Keegan had been silent. Now he put an arm around Vicky's shoulders. "Let me help, Vicky. Marry me now. I'm not saying that's the only way out of this, but I *am* the county sheriff. The Fosters might be more inclined to leave you alone, once you're married to me."

She looked over at him. "You haven't said anything about love."

"Do I have to?" he said. He was red-faced, because the Kid and Torn were listening. He lowered his voice. "You know I love you."

She stepped out of his hold. "I'm fond of you, as well, Peter, but it's too early after Father's death for me to think of marriage," she said.

"What are you going to do, then? You can't run a place this size with only two people."

"I can try."

Keegan shook his head in admiration. "I guess that's one of the reasons I love you so much. I'll wait for you at the house."

He walked away.

Vicky turned to face her remaining employees. "Thank you for staying," she said. "We have our work cut out for us. The only consolation is, it can't get any worse than this."

Clay Torn cleared his throat. "Actually, it can, Vicky. You'll be running this place with one man, not two."

"I don't understand," Vicky said.

Torn looked from her to the Kid. "I've got something to tell you."

CHAPTER 17

"A JUDGE!" VICKY SAID. "A REAL JUDGE?"

Torn nodded, furrowing his brow. "U.S. District Court. I'm Tom Fleming's replacement."

"Does anyone else know?" she said.

"Sheriff Keegan's the only one."

They were walking down from the grave, toward the ranch house. In the distance, Pete Keegan waited for them. "I thought there was something wrong about you," Vicky said. "You were too...too smart to be a drifter."

Beside them, the Kid said, "I was right about you the first time, wasn't I? You weren't what you seemed. I thought you was a Foster plant, myself. But after that fight at the cow camp...well, I forgot about the other part, and I was just glad to have you with us."

Torn grinned.

The Kid went on, "Strange kind of judge, though, ain't you? I mean, shouldn't you be sitting on a bench, or behind a bench, or something, wearing robes? Not working cattle and swapping shots with the Fosters, that's for sure."

"Justice is where you find it," Torn said. "Anyway, if I do what you say, I may get myself shot to pieces, like Judge Fleming. I also might wait 'til Doomsday to see this county cleaned up."

"But why were you working here at our ranch?" asked Vicky.

"I wanted to get hard evidence on somebody, before showing my hand. From what I'd been able to learn, you Larkins were the most likely suspects."

Vicky stopped. She looked shocked. "All this time you were looking to put us in jail?"

"I was doing my job," Torn explained. "I had to start somewhere. I thought the Larkins had killed the Foster foreman. I thought the Kid had pulled the trigger." He looked at the Kid, then back to Vicky. "I know now I was wrong." He tilted his hat brim back. "That Helpton killing still has me confused. If somebody from the Larkin side didn't do it, who did?"

"I don't know," Vicky said. "That's puzzled us, too."

They started walking again. At the bottom of the rise, the Kid said, "What are you going to do, now, Clay?"

"I've got some ideas I want to follow through on," Torn said. "One place in particular I want to visit."

"Want me to come with you?"

"No. I work alone. Anyway, you're needed here. You're a likely target, now, Kid. 'Til this is over, you best stick close to the ranch house. The herd is sold, most of the ranch work is done 'til the fall round-up. You can just sit tight."

"What about me?" asked Vicky.

"I don't think they'll try to kill you, but to be on the safe side, you keep close to the ranch, too."

"If we don't watch the cattle, some of them are going to drift across Strawberry Creek," said Vicky.

"Let them go," Torn told her. "There's nobody left to ride line, and it's too risky going after them. Better to lose a few head of cattle than your life."

Vicky looked at the Kid. "It's just the two of us, Kid. Can you abide being alone with me for a while?"

The Kid looked down shyly. "Yes, ma'am. I reckon."

"I warn you, I play a mean game of checkers."

"I'm pretty fair myself, ma'am."

"My name's Vicky."

"Yes, ma'am, Vicky, ma'am." The Kid blushed red behind his blond moustache.

"You still haven't told me *your* name," Vicky pointed out.

"It's . . . it's Henry," said the Kid.

Torn looked at the Kid and rolled his eyes.

Vicky turned to Torn. "I thought you told me I wouldn't like his name."

Torn shrugged helplessly.

"I think Henry is a nice name," she said.

"Thanks, ma—Vicky."

They had caught up to Sheriff Keegan. Keegan looked at Torn with raised eyebrows.

"It's all right," Torn said. "They know about me."

Keegan's expression showed that he didn't approve. "I wish you hadn't told Bill Foster that we'd found his pistol," he said to Vicky.

"Why?" said Vicky. "He must have known he'd left it there."

"But he didn't know we'd found it. I'm going to go ahead and bring him in, Judge."

Torn was silent. He could see that the slightly built sheriff was determined to go ahead with the move. He wanted to show Vicky he could be effective at his job.

"I think it's time to see what we can get out of him," Keegan went on. "Who knows? Maybe he'll get scared and tell us everything."

"All right," Torn said. "Just be careful. Watch your back."

"I will," Keegan promised.

Keegan turned and offered Vicky his arm. With a quick glance at the Kid, Vicky took it. She and Keegan walked off toward the house.

Torn and the Kid watched them go. Then Torn turned to the Kid. *"Henry,"* he said, with heavy irony.

"It was the best I could think of," the Kid said. "You have to prepare them for a name like Hans." Then he said "When will you be leaving here?"

"Tonight," Torn said. "There's some place I want to be by first light."

CHAPTER

18

TORN LEFT THE LARKIN RANCH THAT EVENING.
Sheriff Keegan had departed earlier. Torn did not ride in
with him. He didn't want Keegan to know what he was up
to, not yet.

A breeze had sprung up from the southeast. Building
clouds promised rain. Torn rode the grullo. The horse had
given Torn no more problems since he had nearly broken
its neck, and he wanted the best mount available, in case
of trouble. In his coat pockets, Torn had stuffed some
jerked beef and a half-dozen of Vicky's sourdough biscuits.

As Torn rode out, he took a last look back at Vicky and
the Kid. The two of them were now alone, save for Vicky's
maidservant, Maria. The ranch seemed eerily deserted
from the bustling place Torn had first seen. He touched

his hat brim to the young couple. They waved, and he turned away.

He put the grullo into a lope. They ate up the country between the ranch and Madisonville. It grew dark. Overhead, the clouds were solid. There was a damp chill in the air. Torn put on his coat.

He circled around Madisonville. He didn't want anyone to see him. Buck Wingate's "farm" was supposed to be about five miles south of the town. Torn followed the road leading south from Madisonville. Dane Richmond had said there was good water and wood, so the farm must be near the creek. Torn rode slowly, halting from time to time and watching his backtrail, but he was alone on the road.

The first drops of rain began to fall. From close by, Torn smelled wood smoke. A track led off the road toward the creek. By the brief flare of a match, Torn could see that the track was not much used, and then only by horses, not wagons or farm animals. He followed the track, going slowly in the darkness. He was almost on the house before he saw it. A light shone dimly through the surrounding trees. Torn backed off quietly. The farm buildings were nestled between the trees, with the creek behind them.

Torn led his horse to a wooden knoll overlooking the farm. He hobbled the animal and let it go. The rain was falling harder. Torn wished he had a slicker.

He decided to go down to the farm and look around. He left the knoll, approaching the buildings from downwind. He blinked rain from his eyes. The fields were overgrown with weeds. If there had been any plowing done this spring—or at any other time—Torn couldn't see it. This must be the place Dane Richmond had talked about.

He moved quietly, keeping an eye on the house. Then an enormous dog leaped out of the darkness, barking and snarling. Torn stopped. The dog sounded like it wanted to tear him to pieces. In the barn, the horses began neighing and stamping. The dog's barking was so loud that it drowned out even the steady drumming of the rain.

Slowly, Torn reached into his coat pocket. He pulled out a piece of the jerked beef that he'd brought along for tomorrow's meal.

"Here, boy," he said softly. "Come here."

The dog kept barking. Torn heard voices from inside the farm house.

"Come here, boy," Torn said. He held out the strip of beef, so that the dog could smell it. "Come here. That's a good dog."

The dog sniffed the meat and shuffled closer, suspicious. The animal was a huge shadow in the darkness and rain.

"That's a good boy," Torn said. He tossed the meat in front of the dog. After a second, he heard the dog's jaws snapping, as it ate.

At the farm house, a door opened. A man stepped out, backlighted from inside. The man was tall and lean. "Gypsy, what the hell are you barking at?" he yelled.

Torn tossed the dog another piece of meat.

"Gypsy!" called the tall man.

The dog gobbled the meat greedily.

From inside, somebody said, "What is it?"

"Nothing," said the tall man. "He's barking at a badger, maybe. Maybe a coyote. Who the hell knows."

"Barking at his own shadow, most likely," said another voice. "Typical damn dog."

The tall man went back inside, to the sound of rough laughter. Dane Richmond had been right. This was no family farm.

One more piece of tomorrow's food went to the dog, and Torn began backing off. He had seen enough.

He retreated to the wooded knoll. There he kept vigil through the night. The rain fell more heavily. Torn was wet and freezing. He would have fallen asleep, but he was too cold. At one point—it was impossible to estimate how much time had passed—a rider approached the farm. Torn couldn't make him out with the poor visibility. He glimpsed a shadow going through the briefly opened door. The man stayed maybe half an hour, then rode away, in the direction of town.

When dawn broke, it was still raining. Torn sat under the spreading branches of a live oak, chilled to the bone. He would have given anything for a fire.

Below him, the farm's residents were up and about their daily activities—bringing in firewood, watering and feeding the horses, using the privy. Torn counted seven men, including Buck Wingate. He wondered if these were the men who had killed Colonel Larkin. They were rough-looking customers. Torn would have bet there were warrants out on at least half of them. Their horses were blooded stock, as good as you could find—or steal.

Smoke rose from the chimney. The men went inside, presumably for breakfast. Torn dug in his sodden coat pocket and dragged out one of Vicky's equally sodden biscuits. He munched it disconsolately.

Wingate appeared, wearing a yellow slicker. He went into the barn. Soon afterward, he rode out. He passed beneath the knoll and went up the road, toward Madisonville. The others remained. In this weather, they hadn't the look of going anywhere. Torn debated whether to stay here and watch the farm house or tail Wingate. He decided to follow Wingate, if only to warm up a bit. He mounted his horse and started after the big man.

Torn rode hunched over in the saddle. Rain streamed off his hat brim. His coat was soaked. Wingate's trail was easy to follow in the muddy road, for there was no other traffic. Wingate skirted Madisonville, as Torn had done on his way in. He left the wooded creek bottom and was soon on the open prairie. Torn took care to stay well behind him, lest he be seen. Now and again he sighted the big man in the distance. The rain was actually something of a boon, because with the bad weather there was less chance of running into Foster riders.

Wingate's tracks turned back toward the creek. He was heading for the Foster ranch, Torn realized. He was going to work. Torn swore to himself. It was what he'd been afraid of. He would have done better to stay and watch the farm house.

The Foster place was in sight now. Torn wondered whether he should turn back, then he decided to stay for a bit, just in case. There was a small rise from which he could view the ranch. Staking out his horse below the rise, Torn took a position not far from the top, lying down so he wouldn't be skylighted. He wished he had a pair of field glasses. It was dangerous staying here. He could be discovered at any minute, and in this county, that could be a death sentence.

Like the Larkin place, the Foster ranch was built near Strawberry Creek. The main house was a "dog trot" cabin, two small buildings connected by a covered passageway.

There were more sheds and outbuildings than at the Larkin place, and the corrals were bigger. Torn watched Wingate tie his horse in front of the main house and go inside.

Nothing happened for a few minutes. Torn was on the point of leaving, when there was movement from the ranch house. Wingate left with another man. Torn couldn't recognize the other man at this distance. The second man went into the corral, roped a horse and saddled it, then both men rode out. As they passed, Torn saw that the second man was Bill Foster. Wingate and Foster headed back across the prairie, in the general direction of Madisonville.

Torn followed at a distance. The rain had lightened. Occasional gusts scudded across the prairie, blowing in Torn's face, obscuring vision.

About halfway to town, Wingate and Foster met two men. Torn couldn't be sure, but they looked like two of the men from Wingate's farm. The four of them sat their horses, talking casually, as if waiting for something, or someone.

Torn left his horse at the bottom of a swell. He crept closer, watching the four men. He saw one of the newcomers nod surreptitiously to Wingate. Then Wingate motioned at Foster's horse, as if there were something wrong with one of the shoes. Young Foster dismounted and examined the hoof. Behind him, Wingate drew his pistol. Foster looked up. Maybe it was intuition, or maybe he had heard the hammer click. As he did, Wingate shot him in the head. Foster's knees sagged, then he crumpled on his back in the mud. His horse, frightened by the noise of the shot, ran off. The other two men curbed their nervous mounts.

Wingate dismounted and checked the body. Then he climbed back on his horse, and with his two companions, he rode off, in the direction of the Foster ranch.

Torn mounted. He cut a wide circle around Wingate and his friends, and started for Madisonville.

CHAPTER 19

TORN HADN'T GONE FAR WHEN HE SPOTTED ANOTHER rider headed his way. He recognized the compact form of Sheriff Keegan. The sheriff was coming on at an easy lope. Torn pulled up and waited for him. The rain had ended. Overhead, the clouds were breaking up. Shafts of sunlight poked through the grayness, shining onto the muddy prairie.

Keegan came abreast of Torn and reined in. "Judge Torn. What are you doing out here?"

"Coming for you," Torn told him.

"I'm on my way to the Foster place, to bring in Bill."

"There's no need for that, now. Bill Foster's dead."

"Dead?" said Keegan. "What do you mean? How? . . ."

"Buck Wingate shot him. Murdered him."

"Wingate? But Wingate works for the Fosters."

"I know," Torn said. "I saw it happen, though. Not more than thirty minutes ago. I had followed Wingate from his farm."

"His farm?"

"Didn't you know he had one? It's south of Madisonville."

"I knew he had property. An investment of some kind. Nobody lives there, is what I was told. I never even bothered checking the place out."

Torn bit back an exasperated oath. "There's half a dozen men staying there. Two of them were with Buck when he killed Bill Foster. I'm willing to bet they're the men that killed Colonel Larkin. I'll bet the farm is where they met after they split up."

Sheriff Keegan gnawed a thumb nail, considering.

Torn went on. "I'd also bet that Buck, or his friends, killed the Foster's foreman, Helpton. Probably Judge Fleming, too."

"But why?" Keegan said.

"I was right at the start of this. They're playing both sides against the middle. They stirred up a range feud, then used it as a cover to plunder the county. They're reaping a fortune, while everybody blames the Larkins and Fosters, who obligingly chop each other to pieces. I just wonder if Buck is the boss, or if there's somebody behind him?"

Keegan ripped off a piece of the nail and spit it out. "That's right," he mused. "There were eight sets of prints at the scene of Colonel Larkin's killing."

"And somebody visited Wingate's farm last night. I couldn't see who it was."

"The eighth man?" Keegan said.

"That's my guess."

Keegan sighed. "I'd have put money on Bill Foster being Larkin's killer. Glad I'm not a gambling man. Are you sure it was Bill that Buck Wingate shot?"

"It was Bill," Torn said.

"Ed Foster will blame Bill's killing on the Larkins, on either you or the Kid."

Torn nodded. "It'll give the Fosters an excuse to wipe out the Larkins once and for all."

"And Buck Wingate will pick up the pieces?"

"That's the way it looks to me," Torn said. "If you've got any better ideas to fit the facts, I'd like to hear them."

Keegan shook his head.

"We've got our evidence now, Pete. I'll swear out a warrant for Buck's arrest, and I'll testify against him in court. The trial will have to be moved to another venue, and we'll have to bring in another judge, but that can't be helped. Are you going to take Buck in?"

Keegan drew a deep breath. "You're damn right I am."

"Deputize me again, and I'll go with you."

"I never un-deputized you," Keegan said. "Which way did they go?"

"They were headed for the Foster place. Let's try there first. Maybe we can catch them unawares." For personal reasons, Torn was hoping that Buck would put up a fight, but he didn't mention that to Sheriff Keegan.

Torn drank water from his canteen. He checked his revolver loads and loosened the Henry repeater in its saddle scabbard. He had been hungry, but the hunger was gone. It had gotten warm in the sun, and he took off his coat.

Sheriff Keegan checked his weapons as well. "Ready?" he asked.

Torn nodded.

The two men started off, riding abreast. Sheriff Keegan looked unusually grim.

About a mile on, they topped a gentle swell of the prairie. Ahead of them, three horsemen blocked their path.

They were Buck Wingate and his two companions from the farm.

Torn reined in. "Trouble," he said.

"Trouble for you," said Keegan. "Not for me."

Torn turned. Keegan was holding a pistol on him.

CHAPTER 20

"GO EASY, JUDGE," SAID KEEGAN. "DON'T TRY ANY-thing, or I'll shoot. I'm an excellent pistol shot, and at this range, I won't miss."

Torn held his hands lightly on his reins. He looked for a way out, and knew there was none. Ahead of him, Buck Wingate and his two companions were coming forward.

"Reach your left hand across your waist," said Keegan. "Take out your pistol and toss it to the ground, off to the right. Do it slow."

Torn did.

"Now, get off your horse," the sheriff told him.

Torn dismounted, fixing Keegan with his pale, blue eyes. "I never figured you to be in on this," he said.

The sheriff smiled grimly. "People have been under-estimating me all my life. They don't take notice of me, because I'm small and I wear glasses. They don't think I can do things. They think they can push me around. Well, I can do things, and I won't be pushed around. When I'm finished, I'll be the most respected man in Larkin County."

Wingate and the two men rode up. One of the men was tall, dark, and hard-looking. The other had a long, undershot jaw and a small gash of a mouth. Wingate had his pistol out. The other two had rifles across their saddle pommels.

Keegan was in better humor now. "You know Mr. Wingate, I believe," he said to Torn. "These other two gentlemen are my new deputies. It seems I've finally found men willing to help me clean up the county. I was supposed to meet Bill Foster with them, but I saw from the tracks that Buck had been tailed from his farm. So I sent my 'deputies' ahead, and I hung back to find out who did the tailing. I had a feeling it might be you."

"How are you going to explain what happened to Foster?"

Keegan sighed dramatically. "Poor Bill. The official story will be that I sent a message to the ranch, by way of Mr. Wingate, asking Bill to meet me, halfway to town. I told him he could bring Buck along for protection, if he wanted. I'll say that Bill met my deputies and me. I questioned Bill about the pistol found at Colonel Larkin's murder. I asked him if he was involved in the killing. You know how hotheaded Bill was. He started a quarrel. He pulled his gun, and I was forced to shoot him. No doubt I'll become a hero for the deed."

"Foster didn't lose his pistol at the murder site, did he?"

"Of course not," Keegan said. "Buck stole it last week. He planted it there."

"Let me guess," Torn said. "The eighth man at the murder scene was you. The set of tracks you followed into town the next day were your own."

Keegan was full of himself. "I played a good joke on you and that tinhorn gunman, don't you think?"

"I can't stop laughing," Torn assured him. "And the man that visited Wingate's farm last night?"

"Was me," Keegan said.

"I suppose I'm to become another casualty of the Larkin-Foster feud?" Torn asked.

"The last casualty, as it turns out. It seems that Bill and Buck caught you while they were on their way to meet me. You being a Larkin hand, Bill accused you of rustling and hanged you. Buck was reluctant to go along, but Bill was the boss. 'Range justice,' they call it around here. There's a war on, and you rode for the other side. No one knew you were really a federal judge. You might have babbled something about it in your last moments, but Bill wouldn't listen."

Keegan turned in the saddle. Leather creaked. He pointed to a distant live oak. The tree stood alone on the prairie, the remnant of some primordial forest. "That's where you'll be found. You're a drifter, so it'll be a quick burial. Nobody's ever going to see those papers you've got in your boot. And if people come looking for you later— what the hell, we never knew who you were. Now, start walking."

Torn took a deep breath. He didn't want to obey, but what choice did he have? He began walking toward the tree. The four killers rode alongside and behind him, covering him with their guns. The tall, dark-haired man led the grullo. He was behind Torn. There was no chance of snatching the Henry repeater from the grullo's saddle scabbard.

"It's my own fault for telling you who I was," Torn remarked casually. "The first rule is, suspect everyone. You've been trying to get me from the start, haven't you? It was you who had Buck and his boys on the road, waiting for me."

"That's right." Keegan laughed. "I had a letter from the Justice Department that you were coming. And after that, at the cow camp, it was you we were out to kill. Later, that's why I asked you to help me trail George Larkin's killers. It's why I suggested that you trail Buck."

"Setting me up for the ambush," Torn said. "Buck was waiting for me. And when he couldn't kill me, he went back and killed Dane Richmond, the only man who could have identified him in court."

Wingate grinned. "I kind of enjoyed that."

"I suppose this range war was your idea?" Torn asked Keegan.

"Actually, it was Buck's idea. We're partners, you see. We have been since the end of the war. We met in the brush country north of Dallas. During the war, it was a haven for deserters, thieves, and killers, men who rode hard and shot fast. I spent most of the war there. Buck came after he'd skipped from the Yankee army."

"So you weren't an officer?"

Keegan laughed sharply. "There's not much profit in that. I went into the brush to avoid conscription. That was another place where men underestimated me, and some of the ones who did are buried there still. Our whole gang met there. After the war ended, it seemed natural that we stay together. Mr. Haycox, the man you killed at the cow camp, is the first one of us to fall in the line of—um—duty in several years."

Torn trudged along. His boots squelched in the muddy spots. In other places, despite the rain, the ground was almost entirely dry, where the water had drained into the sandy soil.

"How'd you come by that limp, Judge?" asked Wingate.

"I cut myself shaving," Torn said.

"You're a funny man, Judge. You won't be laughing in a few minutes."

"I don't know. I can always have a few chuckles at your face."

Wingate reached a foot from its stirrup and kicked Torn in the back.

The live oak drew closer. Torn saw no way of escape, yet he knew he must fashion one. He flicked his eyes at his captors. Wingate was watching him eagerly, full of blood lust. The dark-haired fellow was alert for anything Torn might try. On Torn's left, Longjaw looked overconfident, as if the deed were good as done.

"So you and your merry men were looting and raping your way across the state, when Buck came up with his brilliant range war idea?" Torn asked Keegan.

"For somebody that's fixing to die, you ask a lot of questions," remarked Wingate.

"Let him go," Keegan said. He was enjoying showing how clever he'd been. "Let him see what he was up against. Then he'll know he never had a chance. First, I had to get myself elected sheriff," he told Torn.

"I heard the other candidate withdrew from the race," Torn said.

"He did. After Buck threatened to kill his wife and children."

Wingate chuckled. "Poor fellow left the county right after that. Can't imagine why."

Torn could guess much of the rest. "So you and your men started stealing Larkin cattle and driving them onto the Foster range."

Keegan grinned.

"Next, you killed Foster's foreman, Helpton. Then you ambushed the two Larkin riders. Each side thought the other was guilty, and the war was on. Both sides could take care of it on their own after that, with an occasional nudge from you if things slacked off."

"Very good," Keegan said.

"Meanwhile, the gang is robbing stagecoaches and travelers, selling stolen cattle and horses, while you conduct investigations that turn up nothing."

Keegan nodded, adding, "And, of course, as sheriff, I was able to obtain information about wealthy travelers, and freight outfits coming through, and express shipments from the banks."

"So what's your idea? Bleed the county dry, then move on?" Torn asked.

"Originally, it was," Keegan said. "Then something happened. I fell in love."

"With Vicky?"

"Yes. Suddenly new horizons opened for me. I've decided to stay here and settle down, become a pillar of the community."

"You plan to marry Vicky and take over the Larkin ranch."

"Not just the Larkin ranch," Keegan corrected. "Now that Bill Foster is gone, my guess is that old Ed will soon die of a broken heart. If not, he'll have an 'accident' in a year or so, after things have died down. He has nobody to leave his spread to, so I'll buy it from the county. I'll be a cattle baron—respected and admired. The man who ended the Larkin-Foster feud. I'll stay on as sheriff if I want. Who knows, the folks around here might even elect me judge."

Keegan laughed heartily at that. So did his companions.

Torn said, "What about Buck and the six dwarfs? What's to stop them from stealing you blind once you're such a big man?"

"We'll be moving on, then, Judge," replied Wingate. "Find us another county to take over. Ole Pete might want to settle down, but the rest of us, we like the excitement. We like the night riding, the gun play. Hell, that's the fun of it."

"And you're just fun-loving boys," Torn said. "It looks like you've got things figured out perfectly."

"Oh, we can make mistakes," said Keegan with mock humility. "When we stampeded Larkin's herd, for instance, the plan was for me to step in and cover Vicky's debts. She would have been mine then. But the herd was saved, so I'll just have to wait a little longer."

They were almost at the hanging tree. Torn had stared death in the face before, too many times. Now here it was again, and he didn't like it. He took a quick look around. Longjaw wasn't paying attention to him. "Can't we make a bargain?" Torn said, trying to sound desperate.

"Afraid not," Keegan said. "You have nothing we want. By the time the next judge arrives, the feud will be over.

The county will be calm again, and that's all that people really—"

Torn whirled on Longjaw. With one hand, he grabbed the reins of the man's horse. With the other, he pulled Longjaw out of the saddle. He vaulted onto the horse and sank his spurs into its flanks, heading for the creek. With a shout, the killers galloped after him.

Torn hadn't gone half a furlong before he realized that his animal was hopelessly slow. He heard hoofbeats behind him. He looked over his shoulder. Keegan was in the lead, uncoiling a rope. Torn lathered his horse with the reins, putting his head low to the animal's neck. The hoofbeats were gaining behind him. Torn veered left, trying to throw Keegan off, but the sheriff stayed with him. Torn turned right. Keegan and his horse matched him stride for stride. Torn spurred his horse mercilessly. He heard Keegan's rope hum. The loop settled over his shoulders. He tried to throw it off, but before he could, Keegan reined in his horse, and took a turn around his saddle horn with the rope's end. The loop tightened and Torn was pulled from his saddle.

Torn was dragged along the ground. He managed to get his hands around the loop. He got hold of the rope and got to his feet. Stumbling, he was dragged forward.

"I told you I could be a good cattleman," Keegan said. "You don't steal as many cows as I have without learning how to use a rope."

Keegan touched spurs to his horse. Torn went down again. His hips and back were torn apart on the rough rocky ground. His skin was pierced by cactus spines— Keegan dragged him through the cactus intentionally. He rolled over. His knees were shredded. There was dirt in his eyes and mouth. He pulled on the rope and tried to get to his feet before he was killed. He succeeded. Keegan urged the horse forward again. Torn went down, and the side of his leg was ripped open. He felt blood mixing with the mud and rocks and cactus thorns. He got up, then went down again. He hit his chin. His teeth cracked together and he saw stars. He'd just missed biting his tongue in half. The backs of his hands and knuckles were scraped raw and bleeding. He wanted to give in, to let go, but he had to hold on. It was his only chance. He got up and fell again, dragged over on his head like an outlaw steer. His scalp was ripped open. Blood ran down his face, into his eyes. He was dizzy from the fall. His body was being smashed to pieces.

Then it stopped.

Torn opened his eyes. Through the blood he saw that they had reached the live oak. He shook his head, trying to clear it.

Above him, Keegan said, "Sort of hate to stop, don't you, Judge?"

"Go to hell," Torn said. There was laughter from the horsemen.

The lean, dark man fashioned his rope into a noose. He tossed the noose over a branch of the tree and fastened the other end of the rope around the tree trunk.

The grullo was brought up. "Get on," Keegan told Torn.

Buck drew the saber knife from behind his back. "I want to work on him a bit, first."

"There's no time," Keegan said. "Somebody might come along and see us. Anyway, it would look too much like torture. You're supposed to be the reluctant accomplice in this, remember? This man was a rustler, or so you and Bill Foster thought. You roped him, dragged him here, and strung him up. Maybe, as he was being fitted for the necktie, he mumbled something about being a judge, but Bill never gave him a chance to finish. Anyway, who would have believed a drifter like this could be a judge? Now, get on the horse."

"Make me," Torn said.

Buck hit Torn in the head with the hilt of the saber knife. Torn sagged. Buck and the tall man dismounted and heaved Torn onto the grullo. With a length of rope, they tied his hands behind him. Keegan looped the noose around Torn's neck and adjusted it.

"Any last words?" Keegan said.

"Yeah," Torn said. "You won't get away with this."

"We already have," Keegan pointed out.

"What are you going to do, Torn? Come back from the dead?" Wingate asked.

"If I have to," Torn said.

The killers laughed.

Keegan said, "You're a card, Judge. I'm going to miss you."

"Speak for yourself, Pete," said Buck. "I'm tired of hearing his big mouth."

Keegan said, "Buck, do you want to do the honors?"

Wingate grinned. He looked into Torn's bloody face. "So long, Judge. Say hi to St. Peter."

With his legs, Torn gripped the horse's ribs for all he was worth.

Wingate lashed the grullo's rump with his quirt.

Torn tried to hold on, but the horse bounded from under him.

Torn swung in the air. The knot hadn't broken his neck like it was supposed to. He kicked vainly in the air. He was strangling. He heard the men laughing, as if he were hearing it from under water. He was turning blue. His tongue protruded. His vision grew dark. He gagged for breath. There was a roaring in his ears. Everything was spinning. There was something that sounded like shots. The roaring grew louder. So did the shots. Then he was falling, falling, into an endless void. . . .

CHAPTER 21

HE WAS DROWNING. . . .

He struggled for the surface, but the surface was a long way off.

He couldn't make it, and he slipped back down, flailing uselessly. . . .

He fought his way up from the depths of a fathomless sea. Light filtered through the depths, and he followed it. He heard moans, and he realized they were coming from him.

The opaque light grew stronger. He was near the surface at last. One more try. He burst through, gasping for breath.

A Spanish voice cried, "Senorita! Senorita, he is awake."

He was staring at an earthen ceiling bottomed with muslin. He was in an adobe house, in the cool shadows of the back room, and he knew that it must be the Larkin house.

He started to move, then stopped, as pain flooded his body. He didn't think there was a part of him that didn't hurt.

He lay on a mattress of sacking filled with straw. The mattress lay on rawhide strips stretched between bed rails. *Somebody's best bed,* he thought. In the bunkhouse, he had slept on a cowhide that he'd unrolled each night.

He was bandaged from head to foot. The bandages were clean, which meant they were changed frequently. He was clean, as well, which meant that he had been bathed. He wondered how long he'd been here, and he had an idea that it had been several days.

With a start, he remembered what had happened to him. He had been hung. By Pete Keegan, Buck Wingate, and two other men. Why wasn't he dead?

"What happened?" he heard a voice croak, and the voice was his own.

A woman's face peered into his. Vicky. That mane of honey-blond hair. That sweet, woman smell. If it hadn't been for Melonie. . . .

"His fever's broken," she said. The voice was cool, smoky.

Another face. The Kid's. The hair a paler blond than Vicky's. Concern etched in his handsome, youthful features. Around the Kid, the smell of sweat and animals and hard work.

"What happened?" Torn repeated. "Am I alive?"

"Barely," Vicky told him. "How do you feel?"

"Terrific. Every part of me hurts."

"I'm not surprised," she said.

The Kid said, "I don't think I've ever seen a man so cut up. Where there ain't cuts, there's bruises. It's unbelievable there's nothing broke. Vicky's been changing the bandages twice a day, boiling the blood out of them. But it's getting better now."

"Is she the one who bathed me?" Torn said.

"Yes," said Vicky. "It's just as well you were unconscious. I had to pick the cactus thorns and rocks out of your cuts, then I washed you down with alcohol."

Vicky and the Kid stood close together, their shoulders touching. "Do you want water?" Vicky asked Torn.

"Yes," Torn replied emphatically. "Please."

With the gourd, Vicky ladled water out of the bucket. She held the gourd to Torn's lips. He sipped at first, then drank greedily. When he'd had enough, he said, "How come I'm not dead?"

Vicky and the Kid looked at each other, to see which one would answer. Then Vicky said, "We followed you— Henry and I. It was Henry's idea. He thought you needed someone watching your back. He didn't want me to come, but I wasn't about to stay here by myself."

"We lost you during the night," the Kid went on. "What with all that rain. By the time we picked up your tracks the next day, you was being tailed. We figured there was going to be trouble, so we kept behind the fellas that was tailing you. The reason we was so late at the end, is that we had to ride wide to find a place to shoot from and not be seen. We didn't want them knowing there was just the two of us."

Vicky continued the story. "When they hung you, we opened up on them from farther out than we had planned.

They shot back, then rode off. The Kid, I mean Henry—"
the two of them exchanged looks again—"had a Sharps
buffalo rifle. You know, the kind with a mile range. He put
a ball through the rope that held you up."

The Kid was humble. "It was luck. I couldn't have made
that shot from five feet, much less a thousand yards. Probably one of their shots went wild and nicked the rope, and
your weight did the rest."

"However it was, I'm grateful to you both."

"After they left, we came and got you," Vicky said. "We
put you over the back of your horse and brought you here."

"How long have I been out?" Torn asked.

"Two days," said Vicky.

"Do they know I'm alive?"

"I don't think so. Henry had the idea of digging a fresh
grave on the rise, in case they come asking about you."

Torn nodded approval. "They must not know it was you
who fired on them. If they did, and they suspected you
could identify them, they'd have come after you by now."

"Do you feel up to some food?" Vicky asked. "I have
broth simmering on the stove for you."

"I can smell it," Torn said. "I'm famished."

The Kid helped Torn sit, propping pillows behind him.
Vicky came in with a bowl of broth and spooned it into
him. Torn's neck hurt. It was stiff, like he'd sprained it.
It was a miracle he hadn't broken it when Keegan's horse
had dumped him on his head. With his bandaged fingers,
he felt the rope burns where he had been hung. Now that
he had a better angle, he saw how his body was patched
and wound with plaster and tape.

"I look like something they dug up in Egypt," he said.

"Judge," said the Kid, "why did Sheriff Keegan hang you?"

"Because I saw his men kill Bill Foster."

Vicky went pale. She put down the bowl of broth. "Bill? Dead? Oh, no." Across her face flashed memories of childhood, of young love, if that's what it had been. Tears formed in her eyes.

"Buck Wingate pulled the trigger," Torn said. "Buck and Keegan are partners. They're the ones behind this range war. Except that there never was a range war. It was Buck and Keegan's gang making you think there was."

Vicky put a hand across her mouth. "Peter Keegan. I can't believe it."

"Believe," Torn said. "Keegan's got plans to take over this county. He loves you, Vicky, but he won't let you stand in his way. He won't hesitate to kill you, if he feels it's necessary."

The Kid had a hard time believing it, too. "Keegan always seemed so . . . so . . ."

"Innocuous is the five-dollar word," Torn said. "He trades on that effect. He and Wingate and their men have taken turns killing Larkins and Fosters, rustling your cattle, making each of you think the others did it. They've been using that as a cover for just about any crime you can think of."

"Then Peter and Buck Wingate killed my father?"

Torn nodded.

"Bill didn't do it?" She wanted to be quite sure.

"He wasn't involved," Torn said.

She let out her breath. "That's good, anyway. Poor Bill." Her expression hardened. "My God, and at one time I thought about marrying Peter Keegan."

"You did?" asked the Kid.

"I said, at one time. He asked me. I had to think about it, didn't I?" She stood. "Damn Peter Keegan. Damn him. I'll..."

"Easy, Vicky," said the Kid, taking her by the shoulders. She made no effort to get out of his grasp.

They heard horses neighing in the corrals.

"Somebody coming," Torn said.

The Kid went to the window. The shutter had been left open on this fine day. The Kid looked out, and he swore under his breath.

"Who is it?" Vicky said.

"Sheriff Keegan," said the Kid. "And two men I don't know."

CHAPTER

22

Vicky joined the Kid at the window. The Kid made a remark under his breath, apparently about Keegan, and Vicky giggled. It reminded Torn that, for all her fortitude, Vicky was just a kid herself.

"The two men. Is one tall and dark, and the other medium-sized, with a long jaw?" asked Torn.

"That's them," the Kid said.

"If they find me here, we're all dead."

"Why can't we take them on, three against three?" said the Kid.

Torn shook his head. "The rest of the gang is just over the rise. I'll wager on that."

The clopping of hooves was audible now. Torn said, "Go outside and stall 'em, Kid." The Kid squeezed Vicky's hand

and went out the door. "Vicky, is there anything of mine in the front room?" asked Torn.

She looked around quickly. "I don't see anything."

"Close the curtain, then. Do you have a pistol?"

"Yes, my father's pistol."

"Give it to me."

She took it from a peg by the front door and handed it to Clay. It was an old Navy Colt, its wooden grips worn smooth. "It's loaded," she said.

She drew the muslin curtain that separated the two rooms of the adobe house, leaving Torn alone.

Torn lay in bed with the pistol. He cocked it. The noise sounded loud in the small room. He fingered it with sweating hands. The pistol was loaded, but when was the last time the loads had been changed, or the caps? Would it fire if he needed it? He realized the back window was open. If somebody looked in. . . .

Out front, the three riders drew up before the house. The Kid waited for them. "Afternoon, sheriff."

"Afternoon, Kid," said Keegan. "Miss Vicky home?"

"She's inside."

The three men dismounted and tied their horses. The Kid moved in front of them, casually. "Any luck finding the colonel's killers?"

"That's what I want to talk to Miss Vicky about," Keegan said. His tone implied that the Kid wouldn't be privy to the information. Keegan stepped around the Kid and onto the gallery, while the other two waited by the horses.

"We're doing all right running the ranch, so far," volunteered the Kid.

Keegan turned, "What? Oh, that's good."

Inside the house, Torn heard Vicky say, "Damn." The curtain to the back room opened. Torn's hat was flung inside. Then the curtain closed again.

Out front, the Kid stopped Keegan one more time. "Can I turn your horses into the corral, sheriff?"

"Thanks, Kid, but we won't be here that long," said Keegan.

Just then, Vicky came to the front door. "Peter," she said. "How nice to see you."

Keegan removed his hat. "Hello, Vicky. These are my new deputies. Mr. Simms," he indicated the tall, dark man. "And Mr. Dawkins," he indicated Longjaw.

The two deputies nodded. "Ma'am," they said.

To Keegan, Vicky said, "You've never had deputies before."

"They're cousins," Keegan replied, "new in the county. They haven't had time to be scared off yet."

"Is this a social call or business?" Vicky said.

"Business, I'm afraid. Do you mind if we go inside?"

Vicky showed him the door.

"Wait here, boys," Keegan told Simms and Dawkins.

"Where's the water, miss?" Dawkins asked.

"Oh, it's in the house," Vicky said. "I'll get it."

She followed Keegan inside. "Excuse me," she said. She stepped through the muslin curtain and picked up the water bucket. She looked for the gourd. Torn stuck it in the bucket with a faint plop. Vicky gave Torn a look, then stepped back outside and handed the bucket to the deputies. "Thanks, ma'am," said Dawkins. The Kid had wandered off to the corral, ostensibly to work the horses.

Back inside, Keegan was looking around the front room. Vicky looked, too, to see if there was anything of Torn's that she had missed. Behind the curtain, Torn lay with his finger around the trigger guard of the cocked pistol. If Keegan came through that curtain, Torn would shoot him.

"Will you sit?" Vicky said.

"No, thanks," Keegan said. "I have a disagreeable duty, Vicky. I wanted to come and tell you earlier, but I've been busy."

Busy looking for me, Torn thought.

Keegan toyed with the lamp on the table. He said, "Two days ago, I had to visit Ed Foster. It wasn't a pleasant visit. I had to tell him that Bill was dead."

Vicky tried to duplicate her reaction when she'd first heard the news. "Bill? He's dead?" She looked out the window, as though in sorrow and remembrance.

"I shot him," Keegan said.

Vicky turned. "What!"

"He drew a gun on me, Vicky. I had no choice. I met him halfway to town, to question him about your father's death. I guess he figured that the game was up. He tried to shoot his way out."

Behind the curtain, Torn was sweating beneath his bandages. He was uncomfortable. He wanted to move, to shift his weight, but he couldn't risk making noise. Outside, he heard footsteps. It was Simms and Dawkins, looking around for sign of him. He tightened his grip on the pistol.

In the front room, Keegan went on. "I won't say that telling Ed was the hardest thing I've ever done, but it came darn close."

"How did he take it?" Vicky said.

"How do you think? At first he flew into a rage. For a moment I thought I'd have to shoot *him*. Then he calmed down, and he started crying. I'll tell you, it gave me chills to see that tough old bird cry. Fortunately for me, Buck Wingate had been with Bill when it happened. Buck backed up everything I'd said. He told Ed I'd fired to save myself. Finally, Ed just walked off. 'Excuse me,' he said. 'I'd like to be alone.'"

Vicky sighed. It was hard to keep from revealing her true feelings. "That poor family."

"Bill rode the crooked trail. He paid the price."

Keegan fiddled with the curtain. He might have wondered why it was closed. Behind it, Torn pointed the revolver.

Then Keegan said, "That broth smells good. Someone sick?"

"It's me," Vicky said hastily. "It's a . . . it's a female problem."

"Oh," said Keegan. He let go of the curtain. "Vicky, where is Judge Torn? I've got to tell him about this."

"Then you don't know?" she said. "Judge Torn is dead. He was hanged."

"Hanged?" Keegan's face registered shock. Vicky had to hand it to him, he acted his part well.

"Foster men did it, I guess," Vicky said.

"When was this?" Keegan's voice was barely a whisper.

"Two days ago. The same day you . . . you shot Bill. My God, you don't suppose Bill was responsible, do you?"

"He was capable of it," Keegan said. "Who found the body?"

"The Kid and I. The judge had gone out on his own. The Kid and I got worried when he didn't come back. We went looking for him. We found him yesterday, on Foster range. He'd been dead for about a day. He'd been frightfully beaten, as well. We brought back his body and buried it on the rise. There's been a lot of graves dug there lately."

Keegan sighed and shook his head. "The poor fool. I told him to give up this undercover act. I warned him something like this might happen." He looked out the window, toward the corrals. "I see you brought his grullo back, too."

"How do you know he rode the grullo that day?" Vicky knew she shouldn't have said it, but she couldn't help it.

Behind the curtain, Torn swore silently. *Don't give it away now*, he thought.

Keegan turned back, momentarily confused. "I . . . it was his favorite, wasn't it? It seemed that's the one he'd have taken."

Vicky nodded. "Yes. As a matter of fact, he did."

A shrewd look crossed Keegan's eye. Vicky knew he was wondering if she and the Kid were the ones that had shot at him and his men. Then the look dropped, and Keegan said, "Vicky, have you given any thought to what I asked you?"

"Yes," she said, "but so much has happened—is still happening. I can't get my thoughts together, knowing that at any time I might be the target for a bullet. I mean, I'm the only one left here—outside of the Kid."

"Something tells me the range war is over," Keegan said. "It ended with Bill Foster's death. I believe he was the prime motivator."

"Why?"

"Who knows? Maybe it was a way of getting power. His father didn't give him enough to do running the ranch. Maybe he got into mischief just to get out of the old man's shadow. It's been known to happen."

"Who killed Helpton, then?"

"I guess we'll never know. It could have been one of your men, thinking they did you a favor, and they never told you. It might have been Bill himself, to get the range war started. Or maybe he didn't like Helpton, held a grudge against him, and saw this as a way to pay him back. Like I said, we'll never know."

He took her arms. "I know one thing, though, Vicky. I love you, more than anything in the world. I want to marry you. I don't want to wait."

He tried to kiss her. She turned her head. She struggled to hide the loathing that swept over her at his touch. "This ranch," she said, "it's a big responsibility."

"I'd like to help you with the responsibility," he said.

I'll bet you would, Torn thought, behind the curtain.

The words that Vicky wanted to say stuck in her throat. Instead, she said, "I can't answer you yet, Peter. You've got to give me more time."

"I won't give you much," he said.

"That almost sounds like a threat."

Again, the shrewd look flashed in Keegan's eye. "Did it?" he said. "I'm sorry. I didn't mean it that way."

"I'm sure you didn't."

"I must be going," he said. "I'll be back. Soon."

"Yes," she replied, noncommittal.

Keegan put on his hat and left the house. He and his two deputies mounted up. Vicky stood in the doorway, watching them. Keegan tipped his hat to Vicky, then the three men turned their horses and rode off.

Behind the curtain, Torn at last shifted in the bed, with relief. He let down the pistol's hammer. Vicky came back from the door and opened the curtain.

"I'm sorry," she said. "I know I almost gave it away, but it was all I could do not to tell him what I knew. It was all I could do not to..."

"It's all right," Torn told her. "They're going to figure out it was you and the Kid that fired on them, anyway. You must be high on their list of suspects."

Just then, the Kid came in from the corrals. "They're going up the rise," he said. "They're checking out your grave."

"They want to see if it's really there," Torn said. "It won't be long before they're back, and when they come, it'll be with guns blazing."

"So what do we do?" Vicky said.

"It's what *I* do," Torn said. "I'm the judge. It's time for me to start dispensing justice."

CHAPTER

23

"**WHAT KIND OF JUSTICE ARE YOU TALKING ABOUT?**" said the Kid.

"The personal kind," Torn replied grimly.

"How are you going to do that?" Vicky said. "You can't even get out of bed."

"A minor obstacle," Torn said. He tried to move, and was overcome by pain again. His vision went momentarily gray.

"Give me a hand up, will you?" he said.

The Kid eased Torn to the side of the bed. Beneath his bandages and bruises, Torn's tanned face went pale. He steadied himself. He stayed that way a second, then nodded. The Kid and Vicky braced him, and he stood.

"Is the house swaying, or is it me?" Torn said.

"Come on, Clay," said Vicky. "You're in no condition to cross the room, much less take on eight armed men."

"There's no time to heal. Keegan and Wingate are going to figure out it was you and the Kid that saw them hang me. They're going to hit you like the Yankees hit Atlanta. The only reason they haven't done it already is that Keegan still thinks you might marry him."

"I thought the key to his plan *was* me marrying him," Vicky said.

"I told you he wouldn't let that get in his way. I'm sure he has a fallback plan. Probably he and his men will wipe out this place, then blame it on Ed Foster. They'll phony up evidence to convict Ed—they've had experience with that, remember. Who knows, Keegan might be forced to shoot Ed in 'self-defense,' just like he shot Bill. Then there will be two ranches he can buy from the county."

Torn took a step. His legs went out from under him. The Kid and Vicky kept him from hitting the floor.

"First step's always the hardest," Torn assured them. "It's all downhill from here."

He took another step. He licked his lips. Another step. "See? You can't even notice my limp any more."

He motioned them to let him go. He staggered to the front door on legs as wobbly as a newborn fawn's.

He stopped at the door, bracing himself. He was dizzy. There was fresh blood on his bandages.

"Clay. . . . " Vicky began.

"I'll be all right."

"Oh, sure. With a little help, you might even be able to get on your horse."

He ignored that. "I need weapons. Do you have a shotgun here?"

"There's a sawed-off ten-gauge. My father carried it when he was a Ranger."

"Perfect," Torn said. "You have ammunition for it?"

"I think so."

"I need a couple of pistols, too. Kid, I'd appreciate it if you would feed and saddle the grullo. I don't want to disappoint Sheriff Keegan with my choice of horses."

"All right," said the Kid. "Anything else you need?"

"Yes," Torn said. "Plenty of jerked beef."

A bit later, Torn sat on the front gallery, cleaning and loading the pistols. Besides the Navy Colt, he had a .44 with the chambers bored through to accept the new metallic cartridges. The sawed-off shotgun, cleaned and lightly oiled, leaned against the side of the house. Torn wore new clothes. He'd eaten and shaved as best he could. Vicky stood beside him, looking worried. The sun was lowering; the shadows were long. The grullo had been saddled and was tied before the house.

The Kid rode down from the rise. He'd been on a scout of the neighborhood. "No sign of them anywhere," he said, dismounting. "They're gone."

"They'll be back," Torn said.

Torn looked stronger than he had earlier in the day. "Are you sure you don't want me to go with you?" the Kid asked.

"I'm sure," Torn said. He looked up, and there was a twinkle in his pale, blue eyes. "Kid, how'd you like to be sheriff?"

"Me?" asked the Kid. "Could that happen?"

"It already has. I just appointed you. I wrote it out on paper. You'll find it in the house."

"I . . . I don't know what to say."

"Don't say anything." Torn sighted down the barrel of the .44. He thumbed the hammer back several times, hearing the oily click of the cylinder.

Vicky said, "Judge Torn—Clay—you don't have to do this. You've got evidence against these people now. You can go to the state's attorney in Austin. You can get warrants against them."

Torn lowered the pistol. "By the time I got through all that government fooforaw, you two would be dead. Either that, or this bunch would be out of the county. Maybe both."

Vicky persisted. "But this isn't part of your job. Why are you doing it? What do you get out of it?"

Torn's eyes narrowed. They took on a faraway look. "Sometimes, doing right is its own reward. I've seen enough injustice to last me a lifetime. I'd like to do my bit to balance the scales."

Vicky cocked her head. "This has something to do with that girl you're looking for, doesn't it?"

"A bit," Torn admitted. "There's other things, too."

The Kid shook his head. "I don't think I'd want to come into your court."

"Why?" Torn said. "If you were innocent, you'd have nothing to fear."

"What if I was guilty?"

"Then you'd be in trouble."

"You a hanging judge?"

Torn holstered the two pistols. "Believe it or not, I don't like to order a man hung. I don't enjoy seeing the sentence carried out. But sometimes hanging is needed to bring justice. Take Pete Keegan, for instance. I know for a fact that Keegan is involved in three murders—I would have made Number Four—and I'm sure there's more. What would happen if I got Keegan in my court, and I sentenced him to life instead of hanging? Keegan's articulate, he looks mild mannered, and he's got a certain amount of charm. Before long, the sob sisters and the Polly Prys would pick up his story. They'd fall all over themselves feeling sorry for him, trying to figure out how a nice fellow like that could go wrong. They'd blame his parents, they'd blame the legal system, they'd blame society. Heck, they'd even blame his victims. Soon they'd be agitating to get his sentence reduced, getting up petitions. Keegan would start giving newspaper interviews, telling how he'd been misunderstood, telling how his life had been bad, but now he'd been seen the error of his ways. Next, you'd have a bunch of fancy-pants Yankee politicians getting on his bandwagon. Keegan's cell would become a tourist stop for every do-gooder east of the Mississippi. Eventually, they'd put enough pressure on the judicial system that Keegan would be let go. And he'd start doing it all over again. More people would die. More people would lose their property. I've seen it happen a hundred times, and to me, it isn't justice. In my court, men like Keegan get what's coming to them."

Torn stood, bracing himself on the gallery porch. "There. That's the longest speech I've given since the surrender at Appomattox." He looked at the sky, golden with twilight. "Time to be going."

"What if you don't make it back?" Vicky said.

"There's an affidavit in the house, along with the Kid's—Henry's—appointment as sheriff. If I'm not back by noon, you and the Kid take that affidavit and light out for Austin.

Give it to the state's attorney. Don't stay here, whatever you do."

Clay slipped the store of jerked beef inside his shirt. He stuffed spare ammunition in his pockets. He mounted the grullo, balancing the shotgun across his saddle pommel. He looked down at Vicky and the Kid. They were holding hands.

"This time, don't follow me," he told them.

He turned the horse and rode off.

CHAPTER 24

THE NIGHT WAS CLEAR. A SLIVER OF MOON CAST
faint light on the wooded knoll overlooking Buck Wingate's
farm.

Clay Torn had been on the knoll for several hours. His
eyes had grown accustomed to the darkness. He had spent
the time waiting, and watching.

The gang was all inside the house, as far as Torn could
tell. He heard distant laughter. From time to time, one of
the men would emerge to use the privy. Occasionally, Torn
saw the dog, sniffing around the house and outbuildings.
On the knoll, all was quiet, save for the occasional whirring
of insects. There were the smells of flowers and new
growth, the smell of the horse that was staked out behind
him.

The ride from the Larkin ranch had tired Torn. He had used his time on the knoll to rest and recover his strength. His neck was in pain. His bandages were wet in places, where blood had begun seeping through. His knuckles were raw and painful. He flexed his fingers, wincing with pain, getting them ready for what was to come. Every now and then, a wave of dizziness swept over him. He could still feel the hangman's noose around his neck. He could still feel himself strangling, could feel himself kicking desperately in the air. The feeling made him shudder and want to be sick.

He decided that he had waited long enough. The men inside the house would be tired. With any luck, they would be drunk, as well, and their reflexes slowed. He wondered if Buck Wingate was there tonight. He hoped that he was.

He rose stiffly, letting the by-now-familiar wave of pain and dizziness wash over him. He picked up the sawed-off shotgun, and started off the knoll. He went slowly, letting his muscles warm up, letting his aching body get used to the idea of movement again. He was downwind, so as not to alarm the horses.

He crossed the overgrown fields. The laughter of the men inside the house grew louder. He caught the buzz of their conversation.

At the edge of the field, he squatted. In a whisper, he said, "Gypsy! Gypsy! Here, boy. Here, boy."

He hoped the men in the house wouldn't hear. "Come on, Gypsy. I've got something for you. Come on. Where are you, you stupid dog?"

Then the dog was there, not twenty feet away. The scant moonlight revealed its outline in the darkness. It was staring in Torn's direction. The animal was silent, the kind to watch out for. Torn hoped it remembered the sound of his voice. He hoped it didn't leap at him and try to rip out his throat.

"Here," Torn whispered, "look what I brought you." He held out the jerky, letting the dog get its smell, as he had done before. The dog took a step forward. Its tail wagged tentatively.

Torn broke off a piece of the meat and tossed it in front of the dog. The dog's jaws snapped as it gobbled the meat down. Torn threw down another piece, closer to himself, this time. The dog moved forward and ate. Torn dropped another piece, right at his feet. The dog crept up and took it. Next, Torn held a piece of the meat in the palm of his hand. The dog sniffed all around, warily. Then, deftly, it took the meat from Torn's hand. Torn held out the empty hand, let the dog sniff it. He petted the animal. "Good boy, Gypsy." He took the entire stock of jerky from his shirt and spread it on the ground for the dog.

"Here you go. Make a pig of yourself."

The dog began eating, oblivious as Torn headed for the house.

The building was a frame shack. In the front room, a coal-oil lantern hung from a ceiling hook. Torn tested the planks of the porch, then stepped up. There was no glass in the windows. He could hear the voices of the men inside.

"I'll see you ten, and raise you ten," somebody said.

There was the clatter of coins, and somebody else said, "Call."

"Pass that bottle, Mulvey," said a voice.

"Don't drink too much, Dawkins," said a voice that sounded like the tall, dark, gunman Simms. "You heard Buck. We got work tomorrow."

Long-jawed Dawkins said, "It's only a girl and that tin-horn gunman. They won't be no trouble."

A harsher voice said, "It's a shame we got to kill the girl. I wonder if Buck'll let us have her first?"

There was laughter, then Simms said, "Buck might, but Pete won't. Pete's funny about that kind of thing."

"So? I ain't scared of Pete," said the harsh voice.

"You ain't got your brains screwed on right, then. Remember what happened to Franklin and Dobie, and them other fellas that gave him a hard time?"

Dawkins swore. "Are y'all going to deal another card, or are we going to sit here jawing all night?"

Torn eased back the hammers of the shotgun. He loosened his pistols in their holsters. He braced himself in front of the door. *I'm going to look like a damn fool if they've got this barred on the inside*, he thought.

He took a deep breath. Then he raised a foot and kicked the door open.

The door swung inward with a crash. The six men in the room turned. Five were seated, one was standing. Cards and money were dropped. Somebody knocked over a tin cup, and whiskey spilled across the table.

Torn stepped inside, shotgun ready. Simms and Dawkins recognized him, and their jaws dropped in shock. There was a red-haired fellow, with no shirt and his chest bandaged. Several of the others bore recent wounds, as well, from the fight at the cow camp.

"Who the hell are you?" demanded a sallow-faced older man, the one with the harsh voice.

"I'm Judge Clay Torn. And court is in session."

Chairs scraped the floor. Men went for their guns.

Torn pointed the shotgun. He fired the first barrel. The standing man was blasted against the wall. Torn swung the weapon. He fired the second barrel, and Simms disappeared in smoke and blood. Torn dropped the shotgun and pulled his pistols. With his right hand he fired the .44 at Dawkins, who collapsed backwards over a chair. Bullets were flying at Torn now, plucking his sleeves. With his left hand, he fired the Navy Colt at the red-haired fellow, who pitched forward over the fallen table. He swung round and fired the .44 at the older man, who slammed into the cupboard. The sixth man crashed through the back door, knocking it off its hinges. Torn fired both pistols at him, missing.

Torn raced out the back door, after the fleeing outlaw. Ahead of him, came two flashes, and gunshots to go with them. There was the sound of a body falling. Then silence.

Torn stopped. A second later, the Poker Chip Kid emerged from the darkness. He held a smoking pistol, and he was grinning.

Torn said, "Son, you're going to get yourself killed, skulking around in the dark like that. I thought I told you not to follow me."

"Hey," said the Kid, "I'm the sheriff now. I've got to investigate this suspicious behavior of yours."

Torn's pulse was pounding. The keening excitement of battle rose in him. He exulted in it, and he wanted more, even as he hated himself for feeling that way. His pains were gone as though they had never existed.

He returned to the house. Inside there was smoke and blood and smashed furniture. Blood dripped from the walls. Bodies were sprawled in all attitudes. Several of the outlaws were wounded. There were moans, cries of pain and shock.

Torn's eyes stung from the smoke. He looked around, disappointed that Buck Wingate had not been here. He bent over long-jawed Dawkins, who was groaning softly, rolling from side to side with pain. There was a hole in his chest where the .44 slug had gone through.

"Doctor," Dawkins moaned to Torn. "Get me a doctor."

Torn grabbed Dawkins by the collar and yanked him up. The outlaw gasped with pain. Torn's pale eyes were alight. "I'll get you a doctor," he said. "First, you tell me who killed Judge Fleming."

CHAPTER 25

PETER KEEGAN WAS GOING OVER THE COUNTY TAX rolls. Collecting taxes was one of Keegan's duties as sheriff, and since he got a percentage of what he brought in, he tried to make sure the rolls were up to date. The income was nothing compared to what he had made so far from the Larkin-Foster "feud," but Keegan liked to get every penny that was owed to him.

He sat in the parlor of his house, behind the main street. It was a four-room house, with a neatly painted picket fence. The rent was paid by the county. Keegan was a man of fastidious habits, and his Mexican cleaning woman had little to do. The kitchen was kept dark. Keegan took all his meals in town. After years of eating beside campfires, it was a luxury he allowed himself. Besides, he had the money now.

He felt at home in this house, after his years in the brush, moving from camp to camp. He didn't think he'd like the small adobe house at the Larkin place. He'd like the Foster's dog-trot cabin even less. For all their money, these ranchmen lived under appalling conditions. No matter, Keegan didn't intend to be in either place for long. Once he took over the Foster ranch, he would build a new house. It would be a mansion, with imported furniture, glass in the windows, and a shingle roof.

No matter what happened between him and Vicky, Keegan was determined to stay in Larkin county. He was going to be a rancher. He was going to have the respect and prestige that had eluded him all his life. He loved Vicky, but she wasn't the only woman in the world. As rich as he was about to become, he could buy a wife if he wanted. All his dreams were about to be realized.

And yet. . . .

His thoughts kept returning to Buck Wingate, and to what the late, unlamented Judge Torn had said about him. Once this range war was finished, would Buck and the boys really move on? Keegan had always trusted Buck before, but now he was not so certain. This county had been easy pickings. In spite of what Buck had said, he and the gang might be reluctant to leave for some place where the danger would be greater and the rewards less.

Perhaps, Keegan thought, *Buck and the rest of the gang should be eliminated.* Yes, that might be wise. He began to think how the job might be. . . .

Clunk-clunk. Clunk-clunk.

What was that?

Keegan turned in his chair. It had sounded like a cowbell.

Clunk-clunk. Clunk-clunk.

There it was again. It was a cowbell. Out behind his house.

Clunk-clunk. Clunk-clunk. Clunk-clunk.

Thoughts of Judge Fleming, and how they had killed him, flashed through Keegan's mind. He took off his glasses and set them on the table. He fetched his pistol belt from the wall peg and buckled it on. He got his sawed-off shotgun and loaded it.

Clunk-clunk. Clunk-clunk.

The noise was coming from the backyard. If this was a set-up, whoever was behind it would be expecting to see Keegan come out the back door. Instead, he pushed open the front door, and stepped silently through it.

Clunk-clunk.

Lights from the nearby main street provided good visibility, even at this late hour. Keegan stepped over the picket fence. Shotgun cocked, he circled around the house and came up on the rear of the yard.

There was no one there.

Keegan lowered the shotgun, sweating.

Clunk-clunk.

Keegan whirled. Clay Torn stood before him. There was a cowbell in Torn's left hand. Torn's right hand hung loosely by his holstered pistol.

Torn rang the bell once more. *Clunk-clunk.*

Keegan's eyes opened wide with astonishment. "You!" he hissed.

"I told you I'd come back from the dead," Torn said. "I have a question. My old gray horse—did you ever give it to that Mexican woman and her kids?"

Keegan was puzzled. "Yes, I did. Why?"

"I wanted to see whether you'd die quick, or whether you'd die slow."

Keegan swore, then recovered his composure. "You're not as clever as you think, Torn. I can have this shotgun up and firing before you pull that pistol."

"Want to bet?" Torn said.

Keegan raised the shotgun. Torn drew his pistol and fired. The bullet hit Keegan square in the heart. Keegan fired the shotgun at the same moment, blasting both barrels into the ground.

Keegan dropped the shotgun. He turned around, took two steps toward his back porch, and pitched onto his face.

CHAPTER 26

THE NEXT MORNING, TORN AND THE KID RODE OUT to the Foster ranch. Torn was drained after the events of the previous night. What was coming seemed anticlimactic. He ached all over. His cuts and the rope burns on his neck stung with sweat on this warm day.

Several miles from the ranch house, they were met by Foster riders, with drawn rifles. Torn and the Kid halted their horses. They put up their hands as the Foster men rode up.

"We don't want trouble," Torn said. "We've come to talk to Ed Foster."

"The sheriff send you?" said one of the cowboys, a freckle-faced youngster. Perhaps he remembered how close Sheriff Keegan had seemed to the Larkins at Colonel George's funeral.

"The sheriff's dead," Torn told them. "So are the men who've been killing your riders and stealing your cattle. All but one."

"Now, we'd like to see Ed Foster," said the Kid.

The cowboys hesitated. "All right," said their leader. "But any tricks, and you won't live to do the laughing."

"No tricks, boys," Torn assured them. "The war's over."

The Foster riders escorted Torn and the Kid. They found Ed Foster alone, riding the western part of his range, surveying its vastness, a figure of solitude and grief. He turned as they came up, and he stiffened as he saw who his men had brought with them.

The elder Foster seemed to have aged since his son's death. There was a stoop to his shoulders, and his once iron jaw had slackened. He still had fire, though. "What do you mean, bringing them here?" he demanded of his men.

The freckle-faced cowboy replied, "They said they had to talk to you, boss."

"I've nothing to say to them," Foster growled.

Quietly, Torn said, "We have something to tell you, Mr. Foster."

With one hand raised to show his peaceful intentions, Torn reached the other hand into his shirt. He pulled out his credentials and letter of appointment, and he handed them to Foster. "Read these. They will explain who I am."

The cattle baron held the papers at arm's length, trying to focus on them properly. When he was done reading, his craggy face registered astonishment. "Is this true?"

"It's true, sir," said Torn. "I've appointed the Kid, here acting sheriff."

"Where's Sheriff Keegan?" Foster said.

"He's dead, and we have a warrant for the arrest of Buck Wingate."

"Buck?" said Foster. "Maybe you better tell me what's going on here, Judge."

Torn told the old man how Wingate and Keegan had started the range war. He told how they had killed Ed's son, Bill, as well as Colonel Larkin and Helpton, and who knew how many others. He told what had happened to Keegan and the rest of the gang. "One of them is expected to live. He's promised to testify against Wingate in return for his own life."

Foster listened to Torn's story first with amazement, then with outrage, then with murderous anger. His heavy brow grew darker and darker. "Buck Wingate, my own foreman. I should have seen it." He let out a deep breath. "I never wanted to believe that George Larkin was involved in all this killing and stealing. Thank God I was right about that, at least. Poor Bill, and George, and all the others." He balled his big fists. "By God, I hope Wingate swings from the highest tree. I'll be happy to help you string him up."

"Where is Wingate now, Mr. Foster?" asked the Kid.

Foster turned to his lead hand, who said, "He's checkin' out them new horses, boss. Then he said he was goin' to Madisonville for the rest of the day, on business."

Foster said, "Ride after him, Barnes. Tell him I want to see him at the house before he goes. Make sure you don't alarm him."

"Yes, sir," said the cowboy. He galloped off, leaving a trail of dust in his wake.

*   *   *

It was after noon when Buck Wingate reined in before the dog-trot cabin. Ed Foster stood beneath the covered passageway between the two halves of the house, amid spare saddles and harness. Buck dismounted. He touched his hat brim with his quirt. "You wanted to see me, boss?"

The Kid and Clay Torn stepped from either side of he house, rifles leveled. "*We* wanted you Wingate," said the Kid.

Buck turned. He swore a surprised oath at the sight of Torn, and reached for his pistol.

Ed Foster was faster. He pointed his Colt at Buck's head. "Just give me an excuse," he said.

"The game's up, Wingate. Keegan and the rest of your gang are dead or wounded. Mr. Foster knows everything. We're taking you in," Torn said.

Wingate saw the heavy odds against him, and he relaxed. The Kid slipped in behind him and took his pistol.

"I thought you was dead, Torn. You got more lives than a cat," said Wingate.

"Looks like," Torn said. Then he added, "I'll have my knife back, now."

Wingate gave him an odd grin. "Think you're man enough to take it from me?"

"What are you talking about?" Torn said.

"I'm talking about a duel, Torn. You and me, Texas style."

"What is Texas style?"

"Something I learned in the brush, after the war. We'll dig us a grave. Then you and me will get in, with knives. Only one of us will get out."

"That ain't going to help you, Wingate. You're still going to hang," said the Kid.

"I don't care. This is personal, between me and Torn. What's wrong, Judge? Haven't you got the guts?"

"I've got the guts," Torn said.

"Then let's do it. If you win, you get your knife back. Maybe you get some information about that girl, too. If you lose . . . well, that's too bad."

Wingate looked smug. Torn wanted to wipe the look off his face.

"Clay, you don't have to do this," said the Kid.

"I want to do it," Torn said.

"You won't mind if I ask your men to do the digging, Mr. Foster," asked Torn.

"Clay—"

Torn raised a hand. "No. My mind's made up."

They went to an open space behind the ranch. Two cowboys, stripped to the waist, dug the grave. It was seven feet long, four feet wide, and six feet deep. The cowboys climbed out.

Torn and Wingate took off their revolver belts and hats. The Kid gave Torn his sheath knife. It was a plain, cheap knife, made in England. There were thousands like it on the frontier.

Smiling through his bushy beard, Buck drew Clay's saber knife. "I'll use this," he said.

"That's not fair, Wingate. It's twice as long," said Ed Foster.

"Let the judge decide," Wingate said with a smirk.

Torn's heart was racing. He just wanted to get started. Everyone looked at him. "Go ahead," he told Wingate. "Use it."

Torn and Wingate lowered themselves into the grave. The sides of the grave were solid. The bottom was muddy.

Torn tested his footing. Only a few feet separated the two men. Torn smelled Wingate's rank sweat.

Wingate looked at Torn with his small, shrewd eyes. "I'm going to whip you, Torn, just like I whipped you the first time we fought."

"Maybe," said Torn, "but this time you can't sucker punch me."

Above, Foster and the Kid and some of the cowboys crowded around. A few others hung back, afraid to watch. "This is crazy!" said the Kid.

"It's a matter of honor," Ed Foster told him. "It's too late to stop it now."

Wingate and Torn faced each other across the narrow space. Wingate held the long saber knife. Clay had the shorter sheath knife. "You called the game," Torn told Wingate. "You make the play."

Wingate feinted with the sword knife. Torn parried.

Wingate feinted again. Again Torn parried. With no room to maneuver, he was under a tremendous disadvantage with the shorter blade. He had let his emotions overrule his head when he'd said that Wingate could use the sword, and that had been exactly what Wingate had counted on.

Torn feinted. Wingate parried him easily. Torn couldn't even come close.

Wingate lunged. Torn turned the longer blade.

Wingate lunged again. Torn turned him again, but Wingate's blade slashed open the back of Torn's knife hand. Torn bit back a cry. He shifted the knife to his left hand.

Torn tried to strike. His blade was easily turned by Wingate's saber. Wingate followed with a sweeping, sideways cut. Torn barely ducked it. He tried to drive his blade up into Wingate's belly, but Wingate countered with a backhanded slash that almost took off Torn's hand.

Wingate slashed again, wildly, backing Torn against the side of the grave. An overhand blow knocked chunks of mud off the grave wall. Torn turned a third blow, but his left shoulder was sliced open. Torn couldn't get his shorter weapon into play. His only chance was to take out Wingate's legs. He threw himself forward, aiming low. As he did, a blow from the sword fell across his back. There was white hot pain, and Torn dropped his knife. He was on his knees; Wingate was partly on top of him. The grave was so narrow that Torn couldn't bring the bigger man down.

Wingate stabbed forward with the sword knife. Torn caught the blade with his left hand. He cried with pain as he turned the blade aside. Wingate pushed down with his superior weight. He drove Torn over onto his back. Torn's sprained neck was wedged painfully against the side of the grave. Wingate shifted his grip on the sword knife. He stabbed straight down. Torn caught the sword hand with both his own. His left hand was spurting blood in his face. His right hand was slippery with blood where it had been cut. Wingate put both hands on the sword. He pushed down, with all his strength. Torn tried desperately to keep him off. Wingate broke through. Torn turned his head; the blade nicked his throat. Wingate raised the sword again. Again, Torn held him off. Torn tried to kick Wingate in the groin, but there wasn't room to get leverage and the blow had little effect. Then Wingate jumped and brought a knee down into Torn's ribs, grinding it as he did. Something gave way inside Torn's ribs. There was terrific pain. His whole body went slack. It was all he could do to maintain some kind of grip on Wingate's sword hand.

Wingate wrenched his sword hand free. He raised the weapon, to plunge it deep. Torn fought upward in desperation, pushing, clawing, burying his head in Wingate's ample gut. Wingate was off balance and Torn knocked him off. They wrestled, and Wingate fell onto his back. Torn's ribs throbbed with pain. On his back, Wingate stabbed blindly with the sword. He caught Torn glancing blows in the shoulder and side of the arm. With one hand, Torn tried to grab Wingate's sword arm; with the other, he pushed under Wingate's chin, grinding the big man's head into the mud and blood at the grave's bottom. Wingate tried to get to his feet. Torn struggled to hold him down.

Torn reached out a hand, searching for the knife he had dropped. He couldn't find it. Wingate stabbed down again. Torn's back was on fire. The pain in his ribs wracked his whole body. Wingate rolled, trying to get Torn off him. Torn dodged another blow from the sword knife. Wingate raised it again. Torn grabbed Wingate's hand in both his own. Wingate clawed the side of Torn's face with his free hand. Torn turned Wingate's sword hand. He forced it down. Wingate resisted. With his last bit of strength, Torn drove the blade into Wingate's stomach. Wingate grunted. Blood squirted. Torn grabbed the sword from Wingate. He plunged it down again. Wingate was yelling. Torn stabbed again, driving the blade deep. The pain in his ribs was sapping his strength. He stabbed one more time. Wingate stopped yelling; he twitched in the bloody mud.

Torn lay across Wingate's blood-soaked stomach. Torn's ribs hurt so bad that he couldn't move. He was exhausted. He heard himself moaning with pain. There was blood all over him, all over Wingate, all over the grave.

Torn rolled off Wingate's stomach. Wingate's chest was heaving less now. The saber knife stuck straight up in it. Wingate's breathing was hoarse. Blood came from his mouth.

Torn sat up painfully. It hurt to breathe. His left hand was practically useless because of the deep sword cut. With the right, he slowly unbuttoned his shirt. He pulled out the waterproof packet containing Melonie's dauger-reotype. Carefully, so as not to get blood on it, he removed the picture. He inched back to Wingate. He propped Wingate's head against the side of the grave. "Now, talk," he said. "South Carolina. Do you remember a plantation called Red Hill?"

"Yeah," Wingate said weakly. "I remember."

Torn shoved the daugerreotype close to Wingate's face. "This is the girl. Melonie Hancock. Did you see her there?"

Wingate's mouth was full of blood. His grin was hideous. "Yeah . . . yeah, I seen her."

"Do you know what happened to her?"

Wingate laughed, and the laughter made him cough blood. "Sure, I know." He collected his breath. "I know where she is right now."

Torn grabbed Wingate's shirt. "Where, you bastard? Where is she?"

Wingate started coughing again, choking. He whispered, "Go to. . . ."

Then he vomited a great amount of bright, red blood. He fell back, and his head lolled to one side.

Tears in his eyes, Torn kept shaking Wingate. "Where is she? Where?"

Someone came into the grave behind Torn. There was a sympathetic hand on his shoulder, and Ed Foster said, "He's dead, son."

Torn let Wingate's body fall against the side of the grave. He carefully rewrapped the daugerreotype of Melonie and put it back in his shirt. Wincing from the pain in his ribs, he pulled the saber knife from Buck Wingate's chest. Clumsily, with blood-wet hands, he unbuckled Wingate's belt and yanked the sword's sheath from it.

Bracing himself against the side of the grave, Torn stood. He placed the sword knife and sheath on the verge of the grave. He tried to climb out. He almost passed out from the pain of his wounds. The Kid moved to help him, but Ed Foster motioned him to stop. This was something that Torn had to do by himself. Torn made it to the top and lay there a second, letting the pain and dizziness pass. Then he stood. His clothes were in tatters. He was cut and covered with blood, his own and Wingate's. He slumped from the pain in his ribs.

Torn looked down at Wingate's body. Wingate had known where Melonie was. Now he was dead, killed by Torn's own hand. After all these years, Torn might finally have found Melonie. Instead, his exaggerated sense of honor had condemned him to continue his long, lonely search. He kicked some of the piled dirt into the grave, on Wingate's face. Then he picked up his saber knife and sheath, and he turned away.

Torn looked at the Kid. "There's one more thing I have to do," he said.

"What's that?" said the Kid, staring at his bloodied friend with dismay.

Torn swayed on his feet, like a drunk. "As a judge, I have the authority to perform marriages. Before I leave here, I'm going to marry you and Vicky."

"Marry!" said the Kid. "I ain't even asked her yet."

"You better get busy, boy. I can't hang around here forever."

Then Torn fainted. The Kid and Ed Foster caught him, and they lowered him to the ground.

CHAPTER 27

THE WEDDING WAS A WEEK LATER. A MEXICAN
seamstress worked overtime to make Vicky's gown and
veil. The Kid wore a suit, paid for by Ed Foster.

The wedding was held at the Larkin house. It seemed
like the entire county was there. They had come to cel-
ebrate the end of the Larkin-Foster feud, as well as the
marriage. A prime steer had been slaughtered and roasted
on a spit. In addition, there were hams, roast turkey, and
fried chicken, along with biscuits, cornbread, pies, turn-
overs, and pound cakes. There was lemonade for the children and women, beer and whiskey for the men.

The young preacher said benediction, but Clay Torn,
wearing a new black suit, and with his left hand heavily
bandaged, performed a civil ceremony. That was the way
that Vicky and the Kid wanted it. Torn was the Kid's best

man, as well. Ed Foster gave the bride away.

When the last "I do" had been said, the Kid and Vicky looked at each other. Vicky was expectant. The Kid scraped his foot bashfully.

"Don't just stand there, boy," Torn told him. "Kiss her."

The Kid looked at the waiting crowd. He licked his lips. Then he swept Vicky into his arms and kissed her. The crowd cheered.

When the newlyweds finally came up for air, Vicky took a step back, catching her breath and blushing. "Wow," she said.

"Didn't realize you were going to stay down there all afternoon," Torn remarked.

The crowd was still laughing and cheering. Then there was a familiar loud barking, and a large black dog bounded up. The dog put his forepaws on Torn's chest. Torn scratched him behind the ears. He looked sideways at the Kid. "This isn't. . . . ?"

"Gypsy," admitted the Kid. "After you wiped out the gang, there was no one left to take care of him. So Vicky and I sort of thought we'd take him in."

"He does eat a lot, though," Vicky said. She looked faintly puzzled. "He really seems to like dried beef."

The dog trotted back to the food tables, where he patiently waited for an opportunity to steal something.

Vicky stood on tiptoe and kissed Torn's cheek. "Thanks for everything, Judge," she said.

The Kid shook Torn's hand. "Yeah. Thanks, Judge."

"Hey, it's Clay to you two," Torn told them.

Ed Foster and Vicky exchanged kisses. "I think you got yourself a good man there, Vicky," said Ed. "If you and Henry ever need anything, you know you can count on me to help. While you're waiting to hire new hands, I'll lend you some of mine."

"Thanks, Mr. Foster," said the Kid.

"Call me Ed, son."

Vicky and the Kid turned away, to receive the compliments of the other guests. Ed Foster stood beside Torn, watching them. "They make a nice couple, don't they?" he said.

"Yes," said Torn.

Foster sighed. "I guess I'll always wonder how it would have worked out if Vicky had married Bill."

"I know," Torn said.

"It's funny, but I sort of feel like those two are my family, now."

"You couldn't have picked a better pair."

Foster lightened up. "How are you feeling, Judge?"

Torn's bruises had started to fade. Aside from his hand, most of his bandages had been removed. "Better," he said. "Ribs are still a bit sore."

The old cattle baron chuckled. "You needed so many stitches, we were going to call in the seamstress to sew you up, instead of Doc Goodman."

"I wish you had," Torn told him. "Maybe she wouldn't have kept giving me that damned Castoria."

Just then, the fiddler broke into a reel. The Kid and Vicky led off the dancing. After a few minutes, others joined in. Those who didn't have partners crowded around to watch.

Ed Foster tapped his foot in time to the music. "You know," he told Torn, "I haven't danced in six years, since my wife died. But damn if I don't think I'm going to find me a partner today. Come on, Judge."

Ed joined the crowd. Torn stared after him, then turned away. He started toward the corral.

They didn't need him here anymore. He had helped bring happiness to Vicky and the Kid. His own happiness was still out there, somewhere in the vastness of the west. He would never rest until he had found it.

Behind Torn, the celebration continued. He mounted his horse and rode away.